Sanskrit Poetics

as a Study

of Aesthetic

Sanskrit Poetics

as a

Study

of Aesthetic

BY S. K. DE

WITH NOTES BY EDWIN GEROW

UNIVERSITY OF CALIFORNIA PRESS

Berkeley and Los Angeles

1963

University of California Press
Berkeley and Los Angeles, California

Cambridge University Press
London, England

*The Rabindranath Tagore
Memorial Lectureship*

was established in 1961, the centenary of the Nobel Prize winning poet of India, to honor the life and work of a man whose contributions to arts and letters were of universal significance, although expressed in terms reflecting his own culture. The annual lectures are devoted to major themes relating to Indian civilization.

The Lectureship is administered by a committee of the Association for Asian Studies, and is composed of members drawn from the sponsoring universities: Columbia University, Harvard University, University of California, Berkeley, University of Chicago, University of Michigan, University of Pennsylvania, and University of Wisconsin.

1961–1962

PATRONS

Mr. and Mrs. Harvey Breit
The Asia Foundation
The Association for Asian Studies, Inc.
The University of Chicago, Committee
on Southern Asian Studies

Host University. *The University of Chicago*
Chairman. *Milton Singer*
Program Chairman. *Edward C. Dimock, Jr.*

PREFACE

In October, 1961, the year of the Centenary of the birth of the great Indian poet and thinker Rabindranath Tagore, a Memorial Lectureship was inaugurated in his honor at the University of Chicago by Sushil Kumar De, Professor *emeritus* of Sanskrit of the University of Calcutta. I am pleased that persons who did not enjoy the privilege of hearing these lectures, on the subject to which a large part of Dr. De's incredibly productive scholarly life has been devoted, now will be able to share his insight and sensitivity.

To my mind, there could have been no more fitting opening for the Tagore Memorial Lectureship. Dr. De is one of the most erudite and wise of India's scholars; his subject is one of importance for those who seek to understand the culture of the Indian subcontinent in its abundant complexity. Nor could there be a more relevant tribute to the name of Rabindranath Tagore than the Lectureship itself. Rabindranath was a man profoundly concerned with all human experience, dedicated to knowledge and beauty. I am certain that he is better honored by fresh offerings of knowledge and by inquiries into beauty than he would be by eulogy. The Lectureship in general and Dr. De's inaugural series in particular constitute an appropriate, continuing remembrance, which has already assisted many in their search for understanding and which will assist many more.

It would be presumptuous of me to try to point out the significance of these lectures to both the study of Sanskrit poetics and our knowledge of the values of a culture so different from our own. Nor need I point out that it is India's foremost scholar in the field of aesthetics who is speaking in these pages. His contributions to his field are well known. But the lectures presented here are, in a sense, unique. They cannot, of course, be divorced from the work which Dr. De has previously done, primarily in his monumental and definitive *Sanskrit Poetics* and *History of Sanskrit Literature: Prose, Poetry and Drama*. In these lectures, however, not only does Dr. De preserve the literary sensitivity which is characteristic of all his work, not only does he treat the history and philosophy of the schools of poetic theory—he also states his own views and opinions on the strengths and weaknesses of these schools. These lectures represent the summation of the thought and evaluation of a subject to which a great scholar has devoted a lifetime.

The value of the work, especially as an introduction to students of aesthetics, has been increased by the notes prepared by Edwin Gerow of the University of Rochester. This study thus becomes the only work in English on the subject of Sanskrit poetics to which a student may go both for a topical and evaluative survey of the field and for suggestive direction as to how to carry his study further.

A great deal of generosity, in time, energy, and financial support, has made the Tagore Memorial Lectureship possible. For their expenditures in these directions, for their untiring efforts in organizing and carrying out the infinite number of small and large tasks which a program like this entails, all of us are grateful to the Tagore Memorial Lectureship Committee, and especially to its Secretary, Professor Richard L. Park of the University of Michigan, to Professor Murray B. Emeneau of the University of California, Berkeley, for his scholarly advice, and to the patrons. Mr. Prafulla Mukerji, Executive Secretary of the Tagore Centenary Committee in America was helpful in every way.

For the success of the inaugural lectures, thanks are due to the members of the Committee on Southern Asian Studies at the University of Chicago, and particularly to its Secretary, Professor Milton Singer, and to the President of the University, Dr. George W. Beadle, who supported the program wholeheartedly.

It was a privilege for the University of Chicago to be the first host university for the Memorial Lectureship, and a great honor to have Dr. De among us, even if for too brief a time.

EDWARD C. DIMOCK, JR.

University of Chicago

CONTENTS

1. Introduction . . . 1
2. The Problem of Poetic Expression . . . 18
3. The Poetic Imagination . . . 33
4. Aesthetic Enjoyment . . . 48
5. Creation and Re-creation . . . 62
Notes . . . 81
Bibliography . . . 113
Tentative Chronology . . . 117

1

INTRODUCTION

IN THE STORY of the birth of the Sanskrit kāvya* given in
the *Rāmāyaṇa* we are told that, having spontaneously pro-
nounced the ādi-śloka,* Vālmīki exclaimed in naïve astonishment: "What is this that has been uttered by me [*kim idaṃ
vyāhṛtaṃ mayā*]?" This interrogation of the Ādi-kavi—*kim
idam*—gives expression to the eternal wonder and curiosity
of the human mind with regard to his own creation. Like the
divine creator in the Hebrew and Christian scriptures, man
as a creator expresses satisfaction and wonders over the
mystery of what he has created. From wonder to enquiry is
only a step, and when the restless human mind sets itself to
solve the mystery his curiosity leads him to open up new
vistas of thought.

Some such mental attitude must have supplied the original motive force which in India brought the study of poetics,
like the cognate study of grammar,* into existence. In the
earlier stages, the older science of grammar was very closely
related to the study of poetics. The earlier grammatical
speculations on speech in general not only prompted rhetorical speculations on poetic speech but also influenced their
method and outlook. Ānandavardhana speaks of his own
system as being founded on the authority of the grammarians, to whom he pays elegant tribute as the first and foremost theorists, *prathame vidvāṃsaḥ;* while Bhāmaha, one
of the earliest known formulators of poetic theory, not only
devotes one whole chapter of his work to the question of
grammatical correctness (a procedure which is followed by
Vāmana) but also proclaims openly the triumph of the
views of the great grammarian, Pāṇini. It can also easily be
shown that some of the fundamental conceptions of poetic
theory, relating to speech in general, are avowedly based on

---

* For Notes, see pp. 81–112. Asterisks in the text indicate items of
particular importance which are discussed in the Notes.

the views of the grammarians, to the exclusion of other schools of opinion. Perhaps the time-honoured tendency of exalting authority and discouraging originality was partially responsible for this modest attitude. Poetics did not think it expedient to appear as an entirely novel system but sought the protection of the grammarian's authority so that grammar, its elected godfather, might help it to ready acceptance.

Whatever may have been the reason, it is well to bear in mind this close connexion between grammar and poetics. Like grammar, poetics started as an empirical and normative study; and despite its later search for fundamental aesthetic principles, it hardly ever succeeded in breaking down its scholastic barriers. Examination of the progress of the discipline shows that although in the course of its advance Sanskrit poetics embraced a great deal more than a mere practical treatment of rhetorical categories, it nevertheless never quite drew away from its analytic verbal formalism into a truly theoretic discipline of aesthetic.

It is no wonder, therefore, that Sanskrit poetics started as a purely empirical, and more-or-less mechanical study. It took the poetic product as a created and finished fact, and forthwith went to analyse it as such, without pausing to consider its relation to the process of poetic creation as the expressive activity of the human spirit. It chose to deal with what was already expressed, never bothering itself with the whys and wherefores of expression; its enquiry was directed chiefly to *kim idam*, and not to *katham idam* or *kuta idam*.* If we turn to the word *alaṃkāra*, which originally was applied to name the discipline itself as well as to designate the rhetorical figures, we find that it signified pure and simple embellishment, taken as a positive or accomplished fact, and hardly had any reference to the process or objective of embellishment.* This forms the main topic of analysis in the earliest extant works from Bhāmaha to Rudraṭa.* They approach the subject as a scientist approaches a physical fact. If any deduction is permissible from these indications, it is that Sanskrit poetics grew out of the very practical object of methodically analysing and classifying the decorative devices of expression by themselves, with a view to prescribing definite rules of composition; and this pedagogic outlook undoubtedly received great impetus from the highly developed analytic enquiry into the forms of language made by the normative grammarians.

It also appears that Sanskrit poetics reached the rank of an independent discipline at a time when Sanskrit poetry, in the hands of less imaginative writers, was becoming more and more a highly factitious product of verbal special-ists.* The tradition of such a poetry both obscured the activity of the poetic imagination and pointed to working the rules and means of external production into an exact system. The result was the elaboration of a series of more or less mechanical formulas and rigid categories. And, in-deed, the *ars poetica* in India, which went by the name of the science of embellishment (*alaṃkāraśāstra*), did not go further than being a series of artificial advices to the poet in his profession.

It cannot, however, be stated that the necessity and in-evitability of postulating an ultimate principle did not at all trouble these early writers. We shall see presently that at almost every step in the history of the study it was almost impossible for the so-called *ālaṃkārikas,** concerned as they were with outward form and technique, to be entirely un-conscious of the theoretic principles underlying literary expression. At the same time, they could never get rid of the idea that words were natural, mechanical facts to be collected in their greatest possible variety and grouped in fixed classes and types. Attention was directed, therefore, to the analysis of the *śabda* (word), with an object some-what different indeed from that of grammar but agreeing in its normative method and ideal. The *śabda* came to be the pivot around which the entire study moved; the question of the function of words in producing different kinds of meaning became the chief concern. It appears to have been thought that, whatever may be the function of the poetic imagination in its expressive activity of finding its own appropriate word or meaning, or whatever may be its theoretic basis, the explanation of the mere verbal arrangement was sufficient for explaining the fact of poetic expression.

That the art of poetry can be systematised, after the method of positive sciences, formed one of the fundamental postulates of Sanskrit poetics from the very beginning. This is what is implied by the term *vakrokti** of Bhāmaha, by which this earliest rhetorician connotes an extraordinary turn given to ordinary speech and denotes the entire assemblage of rhetorical ornaments. His successors, Udbhata* and Rudraṭa, do not employ this generic term, but their attempts, like his, are limited to the systematic classification of expression into more-or-less fixed rhetorical categories. This formal treatment gives their works the general appearance of technical manuals comprising a collection of definitions, illustrations, and empirical canons elaborated for the benefit of the aspiring poet. The standpoint is similar to that of an art of painting which confines itself to a collection of information about the techniques of tempera, oil painting, watercolour, and pastel, about the proportions of the human anatomy, and about the laws of perspective, forgetting that a painted picture is more than a mere ingenious application of such knowledge or device. It regarded poetry as a more or less mechanical series of verbal devices in which a definite sense must prevail, and which must be diversified by means of prescribed tricks of phrasing, the so-called figures of speech to which the name of 'ornament' (*alaṃkāra*) is given. As the botanist or the zoölogist labels and classifies every new representative of flora or fauna, the Sanskrit *ālaṃkārika*, pretending to find universals, calculates the particular species from the original four ornaments of Bharata* to more than a hundred of Jayadeva.* But, in view of the inexhaustibility of individual poetic expressions, they may be easily *renewed* to an infinite number; moreover the universals of a formal analysis are of doubtful theoretic value for explaining the principle of concrete individual expression itself.

The aesthetic insufficiency of rhetorical categories was, however, very speedily perceived; but the theories which were advanced against mere rhetoric did not entirely reject it. On the contrary, a reserve was made regarding its utility, and its principles were carefully preserved. When Vāmana declared that *rīti,** by which he meant a specific arrangement of words, was the essence of poetry, he did not advance the speculation very much further. Nor did his predecessor Daṇḍin give an extended interpretation of the term 'ornament,' applying it to anything which lends 'beauty' (*śobhā*) to poetry, and including in its scope the figurative devices as well as modes or grades of arrangement of word and sense, although Vāmana draws a sharper distinction between the particularities of arrangement and the mere figures of speech. Both of them believe that the modes or particularities of arrangement consist of the combination of certain fixed 'qualities' or 'excellences' (*guṇas**) realised by different dispositions of word and sense, such as 'perspicuity', 'smoothness', 'liveliness', and so forth.* In the formal schemes of poetry of both, these are considered to be of essential importance for the production of poetic beauty; the mere figures of speech, though vaguely admitted by Daṇḍin as common to all the modes, are acknowledged but relegated by Vāmana to a subordinate position as accidental ornaments, which serve to enhance the beauty already produced by the so-called 'qualities'.

It must be made clear, however, that the term 'beauty' (*śobhā*), which is taken as the test of poetry, is not defined; but it appears to have no other far-fetched meaning than that of the logical external effect realised by a carefully worked-out adjustment of word and sense which avoids damaging flaws by adopting, primarily, the literary 'qualities', and, secondarily, the figures of speech for heightening the effect thus produced. The term *rīti*, defined as a specific arrangement of word and sense for the purpose of realising this beauty, thus signifies nothing more than a mere combination, in various degrees, essentially of these clearly defined 'qualities' and incidentally of the figures of speech. It has no reference to the organic expressive activity of the poetic intuition, nor is it equivalent to the English word 'style' as the expression of poetic individuality. It is capable of technical formulation, being the verbal 'diction' in the objective sense.

As such, the so-called 'qualities' of 'simplicity', 'vivacity', and so forth, become only generic or specific categories for labelling particular aspects of the aesthetic activity; they do not explain the character of the activity itself. The 'qualities' properly designate the different degrees in the development, free or less free, of the expressive activity, and are thus aspects of successful or less successful expression. When completely successful, we have the expression itself. The so-called 'flaws' (*doṣas**) designate embarrassed activity, ending in failure, and are thus aspects of unsuccessful expression. From the aesthetic point of view, this success or failure of expression may also be termed beauty or ugliness. But the beautiful, as the perfect expression, does not possess degrees. If ugliness does, complete ugliness, as complete negation, altogether ceases to be ugly; for it loses its contradiction and is no longer an aesthetic fact. The consideration of expression itself, therefore, is important, rather than a scholastic definition of its different degrees of success or failure, of freedom or bondage.

The distinction between 'qualities' and figures of speech as essential and nonessential may, then, be of some use in logical or scientific, but not in aesthetic, analysis. Given a particular expression, the 'qualities' are as much integral parts of it as are figures of speech. The expression should be taken not as a mechanic but as an organic whole in relation to the poetic intuition.* As each expression automatically selects its own appropriate qualities and ornaments, it cannot be definitely laid down that a particular expression should possess this and should not possess that. If expression is expression, it is successful; if not, it is not successful; there cannot be any question of intermediate degrees of success in aesthetic estimate. Nor can generic 'qualities' or 'ornaments' be categorically attached, for expression is not a fixed and generic but a variable and individual fact.

In having drawn attention for the first time to the aspects of poetic activity indicated by the 'qualities', the *rīti-*

theorists may be regarded as having gone a step further than the mere *ālaṃkārikas*, but the speculation in its halting formalism touches only the fringe of the problem. By their very attempt at systematisation the *ālaṃkārikas* recognised the existence of certain facts as aesthetic facts; the *rīti* theorists went further and held that these facts are reducible to a definite principle. But both schools failed to realise that this principle is not an external category but a category of the spirit.* It should have been clearly understood that every single expressive fact stands by itself. Such facts may be grouped generically by the inductive process, but the continuous variation of individual poetic expression results in an irreducible variety of expressive facts. There may be a formal division of grades or modes, but it has hardly any use, except for logical or scientific purposes. Each poet has his own mode characteristic of his particular intuition in a specific case. With such differentiation, the classification of modes would be endless without reaching any definite theoretic principle of expression.*

This has, however, given to Indian scholastic minds rich material for subtle distinctions and opportunity for hairsplitting analysis and definition. Just as there has been a multiplication of limitless varieties of poetic figures as verbal variants in a formal scheme of rhetoric, the objective definition of *rīti* as a particular kind of formal arrangement, a peculiar disposition or posture of parts, easily led to essentially unprofitable attempts at inconstant and capricious classifications. Indeed, Daṇḍin declares that speech is diversified in its mode of expression and shows himself cognisant of the distinctions which mark off one mode from another and result in a multifarious variety of modes. But, maintaining that the subvarieties are incalculable, he distinguishes two generic types, *Vaidarbhī* and *Gauḍī*, and sets them against each other.* His successor Vāmana proposes three types, adding *Pāñcālī*,* and recommending the *Vaidarbhī* as containing all the 'qualities', and subsequent writers add *Lāṭī*,* *Āvantikā* and *Māgadhī*. All are in reality instances of complete and incomplete expression, erected into definite generic types, probably (as the names imply) on the basis of empirical observation of localised usages. In the same way, the 'qualities', like rhetorical categories, were found incapable of fixed and precise definition and were therefore susceptible to considerable multiplication, and the attempt to label, classify, and stereotype the entire poetical output, on the basis of more-or-less formal analysis, into so many ready-made modes and fixed 'excellences' was bound to prove unconvincing as the theoretic basis of poetic expression.

The theorists, who came into prominence in the next stage, consequently declared that the true character of poetry was not understood by those who had cognisance only of the science of word and sense.* But, curiously enough, their own theory had its origin, in the conventional manner, in the analysis of languages and meaning. From grammarians and logicians they acknowledged the functions of denotation* and indication,* the former giving the literal sense of the word; and the latter, the literal sense, being uncompatible, a further secondary but allied sense.* But this is not all. They went further than the grammarians and logicians, contending that denotation and indication do not exhaust the entire significance of poetry. They posited still another function of word and sense, suggestion,* which provides another sense, never directly expressed, but depending upon the poet's particular purpose in employing the word in its obviously denoted or indicated sense.* Here for the first time the poet's purpose is brought into the consideration of the product of the poet's mind, and an unexpressed sense (*vyañgya**) is acknowledged beyond what is directly expressed in so many words.

But the analysis is still empirical, concerned with the form rather than with the essence.* These theorists, no doubt, clearly perceive that the consideration of the ornamental fitting out of words or the literary qualities of structure does not fully solve the problem. They clearly demonstrate that 'ornaments' or 'qualities' have no absolute value, but depend upon the character of the particular utterance. In recognising all this, they sailed very closely along the coast, but they hardly succeeded in making an effective landing. The theory rendered great service by rightly emphasising that the literal sense alone is not sufficient, that it should lead to the deeper, suggested sense of poetry. But the analysis still concerned itself with the intellective rather than the intuitive aspect of a good poem, with the understanding of its ideas as empirical facts. The theory passes from aesthetic to logic and reduces expressive facts into logical relations by subjecting an individual artistic composition to universal abstract formulas. The unexpressed has no reference to the individual poetic intuition, but is universalised as a mode of thought; and, being bound up by definite links with fixed and mechanical symbols of the expressed, it becomes as much a fixed and mechanical universal as any rhetorical or qualitative category.

The attempt, therefore, resolved into the same method of elaborately distinguishing and classifying thousands of varieties of the unexpressed; and even when the unexpressed was generically classed as unexpressed matter, unexpressed ornament, or unexpressed sentiment—corresponding to the earlier mechanical grouping of descriptive, ornamental, and sentimental composition—the speculation still only labelled and pigeonholed certain generic or specific aspects of the poetic function without exhausting or explaining the function itself.

And this was not enough. To say that the unexpressed is the essence of poetry or to analyse into groups the varieties of unexpressed meaning falls short of the main issue; for poetry is expression which contains in itself what is obviously expressed as well as what is implicitly suggested. In aesthetic analysis (as opposed to the merely logical) it is impossible to separate the unexpressed and the expressed —both together make up the being of an artistic composition. The poet's purpose, upon which the unexpressed meaning is said to depend, is not meant to be coëxtensive with his poetic intuitivity, which is rich in unified images rather than in disintegrated thought or meanng, in its power of intuitive expression rather than in presenting this or that particular concept. The expression is the actuality of the intuition, the so-called expressed and unexpressed forming indissoluble constituents, undistinguishable in the organic whole.

To be sure, Sanskrit theory recognises that in order to be poetical languages should be generically semantic, but it forgets that the language of poetry must be taken as one of intuition and not of intelligence, as an aesthetic and not an intellective fact. The pedantic bipartition between the un-expressed and the expressed, therefore, is useless except in grammatico-logical analysis; for the whole constitutes poetry and not a part, and it helps us little to analyse externally what cannot in its internal unity be analysed. The poet's "purpose" * is unnecessarily and narrowly segregated from the word and its meaning, while the poetic purpose in its true sense is the word and the meaning themselves in their unity. The unexpressed meaning is preëminently the poetical and not the logical or ethical meaning; but the poetic intuition knows no dualism between word and meaning, between itself and its expression, for the content here is form and the form is content. In attempting to combat the science of word and sense, the new theory appears to have only preserved the earlier tradition in a different garb, starting with the same presupposition that a word, or its sense, is a natural, mechanical fact, which can, in the manner of a scientific fact, be grouped in classes and types.

This school of opinion* did an important service, however, directing attention to an aspect of poetry which had been imperfectly understood or entirely ignored in Sanskrit theory. Hitherto, speculation had been busy with the consideration of poetical ornament and structure as ornament and structure; and it was thought adequate if these means related certain definite ideas in a definite manner. But the later theorists realised that poetry was not the mere clothing of agreeable ideas in agreeable language; the emotion* (as opposed to mere knowledge) plays an important part in it and can as well constitute the material of poetry as it forms the material of life. A new question arose: How could the emotions be expressed? The later theorists* maintain that emotions are in themselves inexpressible. We can give a name to each emotion, but naming it is not equivalent to expressing it; at best we can suggest it.

Considering the emotions the most vital materials of poetry, the new school took them up as an element of the unexpressed, which they held to be the essence of poetry. They elaborated the thesis that what the poet can directly express or describe with reference to the emotions are the causes which give rise to them (*e.g.*, the situation, the environment, or the hero and heroine as their receptacle). With the help of these expressed elements, which must be generalised and conceived not as they appear in the natural world but as they may be imagined in the world of poetry, the poet can awaken in the reader, through the power of suggestion inherent in words and their meanings, a particular condition of the mind in which a relish of the emotions is possible. The poet cannot rouse the *same* emotion as, for instance, his hero or heroine, the mythical Rāma or Sītā whom he describes, felt. But since all human minds possess germs of the same emotion (here love) in themselves, and since the expressed elements as well as the emotional are generalised, he can call up the reflection of a similar emotion. This condition of the reader's mind in the enjoyment of the generalised emotion is called the relish* or *rasa*, which can be awakened only by the suggestive power of expressed word and sense.

This relish of the poetic sentiment partakes, no doubt, of the nature of cognition. But the theorists are careful in explaining that it is nevertheless different from the ordinary forms of the process, because its means, the expressed factors* which suggest it, are not to be taken as ordinary natural causes.* They hold that, although the relish or *rasa* requires these factors for its manifestation and cannot exist without them, it cannot yet be regarded as an ordinary effect, and the causal relation is inapplicable to this case, for in the spiritual sphere of poetry the connexion between cause and effect gives place to an imaginative system of relations which has the power of stirring latent emotional impressions of the reader's mind into *rasa*. Thus the resulting relish cannot be identified with the constituent factors; at the time of relish, the latter are not experienced separately, but the whole appears as *rasa*, which is simple and indivisible, and from which every trace of the constituent factors is obliterated.

These theorists hold that the emotion itself exists in the mind of the reader in the form of latent impressions (*vāsanā**) derived from actual experiences of life or from inherited instincts. On reading a poem which describes a similar emotion, this latent emotion is suggested by the depicted factors which, presented in a generalised form, cease to be 'ordinary causes' but become 'extraordinary causes' in poetry. The factors, being generalised or impersonalised by the suggestive power of word and sense, do not refer to particularities; Rāma and Sītā are no longer Rāma and Sītā as individuals, but represent the lover and his beloved. Similarly, the emotion suggested, which is the source of the relish, is also generalised; the love of Rāma and Sītā becomes love in general, and it is possible for the reader to relish the emotion in this generalised form, for its impression is already latent in his mind. The emotion (*bhāva*) is generalised into a sentiment (*rasa*) also in the sense that it refers not to any particular reader but to readers in general. The particular individual, while relishing as a reader, does not think that it is his own personal emotion, and yet it is relished as such; nor does he think it can be relished by him alone, but by all persons of similar sensibility.*

Thus, by generalisation (*sādhāraṇīkaraṇa**) is meant the process of idealisation by which the reader passes from his troublous personal emotion to the serenity of contemplation of a poetic sentiment. The poet as well as his audience must possess this capacity of idealisation; otherwise he will never be able to present personal emotion as an impersonal poetic sentiment capable of being relished by others. The resulting relish, therefore, is neither pain nor pleasure in the natural sense, which is found in the ordinary emotions of life associated with personal interests (which word should also be understood to connote scientific interest in them as objects of knowledge), a relish dissociated from all such interests, consisting of pure joy free from the contact of everything else perceived but itself. Put another way, an ordinary emotion (*bhāva*) may be pleasurable or painful; but a poetic sentiment (*rasa*), transcending the limitations of the personal attitude, is lifted above such pain and pleasure into pure joy, the essence of which is its relish itself.

The artistic attitude is thus given as different from the naturalistic and closely akin to but not identical with the philosophic. It is like the state of the soul serenely contemplating the absolute (*brahmāsvāda*), with the difference that the state of detachment is not so complete or permanent. The artistic attitude is thus recognised as entirely spiritual. But the idealised artistic creation affords only a temporary release from the ills of life by enabling one to transcend, for the moment, personal relations or practical interests; it restores equanimity of mind (*viśrānti*)* by leading one away, for the time being, from the natural world and offering another in its place. It is an attitude of pure bliss, detached spiritual contemplation (*citsvabhāvā samvid*), similar to but not the same as the state of true enlightenment which comes only to the knower who, no longer on the empirical plane, transcends completely and permanently the sphere of pleasure and pain. As such, this state of aesthetic delectation is not capable of proof, for its intuition is inseparable from its existence—it is identical with the experience of itself. The only proof of its existence is its relish itself by the man of aesthetic sensibility, the *rasika* or *sahṛdaya*, the ideal connoisseur, to whom alone it is vouchsafed.

The theory, as has already been noted, demands the existence of aesthetic intuition, or capacity for true enjoyment of so-called poetic bliss. But the presupposition of latent impressions is only an aspect of this demand. Those who do not possess this intuition can never relish the spiritual state, and the theorists are merciless in their satire on dull grammarians and mere dialecticians, who are incapable of attaining the aesthetic attitude. It is the *rasika* or *saḥṛdaya* alone, who by his own intuition can identify himself with the intuition of poetic creation (*tanmayībha-vanayogyatā*), and thereby obtain its true relish (*rasa*). It must be understood that although 'relish' or 'taste' renders the word '*rasa*' literally, it does not imply, apart from the idea of the critic's reproduction of the poet's production, any conscious ethical valuation, 'good' or 'bad' taste. It implies an experience similar to what we understand when we speak of relishing or tasting food; but this realistic description must not at the same time drag it down to the level of natural pleasure, because by its aloofness and serenity it is lifted into a personal-impersonal blissful state of the mind. The word *Stimmung* used by Jacobi[*] may give us the nearest approach. But the *rasa* is not a mere highly pitched natural feeling or mood; it indicates pure intuition which is distinct from an empirical feeling.

It is clear that, however blissful, the aesthetic enjoyment, or the enjoyment of the poetic sentiment, as conceived by these theorists, must be distinguished from the enjoyment of natural feelings. And the theory does not fall into the mistake of aesthetic hedonism, which sees no difference between the pleasure of poetry and that of easy digestion. No doubt, the conventional classification of generic and specific feelings is accepted,[*] but they are given as constituting the material or stimulus of poetry. They may form the concomitant or substratum of the poetic sentiment (*rasa*), but are not identical with it. Just as one cannot talk of cause and effect in the unity of spirit, so in the unity of *rasa* the separate natural feelings (*e.g.,* grief, horror, comedy) which may form its constituents, are never experienced. The whole appears as a single and indivisible aesthetic sentiment from which every trace of the constituent empirical pleasure or pain is obliterated. This fact is borne out by the common experience that when grief is experienced on the stage the spectator says: "I have enjoyed it." Viśvanātha[*] explains clearly that tears constitute no proof that pain is felt; for the tears that are shed by the spectator are not those of pain but those of sentiment, due to the nature of the particular aesthetic enjoyment. Hence in a devotee, as

Jagannātha* observes, tears arise on the contemplation of the deity, where the religious feeling is raised to a serene state of similar enjoyment. The intuitive bliss arising from idealised artistic creations should, therefore, be distinguished from the experience of natural feelings and from all natural experiences of life.

It follows that the question of ornament or structure of poetry must be revised and viewed from this standpoint. The poetic intuition automatically chooses its own expression, which is only the externalisation of the spiritual activity and, therefore, not a mechanically fixed fact but a part and parcel of that activity. Ānandavardhana declares that the ways of expression are infinite (*anantā hi vāgvikalpāḥ*), and, since there is no end of poetic individuations, it is futile to elaborate rhetorical or qualitative categories. Only the broad rule can be laid down: they must follow the import of the poetic intuition, which in his theory is the aesthetic sentiment or *rasa* intended by the poet. Moreover, if it is necessary to accept the older conventional categories of rhetorical figures and qualities, the only rule that should govern their employment is their appropriateness to the particular *rasa*. Ānandavardhana, therefore, states very clearly that there is no other circumstance which leads to the violation of the *rasa* than inappropriateness, and that the supreme secret of *rasa* consists in observing the rules of appropriateness. For each poetic creation its appropriate words exist; and the theory of propriety (*aucitya*) alone should explain and justify their employment.

In this, Ānandavardhana shows himself conversant with the essential nature of poetic expression. He rightly explains that the 'qualities' are not mere tricks of sound and sense but should be considered in effective relation to the suggested sentiment of a composition. The consideration of structure as such, therefore, is not necessary, and the distinction between 'qualities' of sound and of sense is meaningless. The spiritual activity involved in aesthetic enjoyment can alone justify them. Thus, it is not necessary to accept the conventional ten or twenty 'qualities'. They may be reduced to three generic ones only, according as they are

the means of expanding, pervading, or melting the mind.*
To be sure, these mental states are often mixed up and lead
to various other mental conditions, but these latter effects
are too many and too indistinct to be made the basis of
new 'qualities'.

This is, in its general outline, the theory of *rasa* finally
reached by Sanskrit theory. The theorists undoubtedly approach the core of the aesthetic problem, but unfortunately
the starting limitations still remain and prevent a proper
development of the theory. Because of these limitations, it
cannot by any means be maintained that they have said
the last word on the subject, or said it clearly and consistently; but they have certainly very ably dealt with some
of its fundamental aspects. A right exposition is given indeed of the aesthetic enjoyment resulting from the idealised
creation of poetry, and incidentally of the general nature
of poetic idealisation. But the question is still approached
from the standpoint of the reader or the critic, the *sāmājika*
or the *sahṛdaya*. The problem of poetic intuition from the
point of view of the poet's mind is not tackled in its entirety. The process is reversed. The theory speaks of the
sāmājika's relation to the poetic creation and goes on to
determine its character as an aesthetic fact solely from the
point of view of its aesthetic enjoyment by the *sāmājika*;
but it does not speak of the relation of the poet's mind to
his creation by starting from the consideration of the
creative imagination and its automatic externalisation as an
aesthetic fact.

With the reversal of the process, the final goal is hardly
reached. Even the new theory could not daringly break
loose from its original barrier. The starting preoccupation
with word and sense remains; and in its attempt to adhere
to their grammatico-logical analysis, the theory loses itself
in the verbal labyrinth of the expressed and the unexpressed.
The process of idealisation is not fully and properly explained; it becomes a kind of abstract enjoyment of abstract
symbols, ignoring the concreteness of poetic intuition and
creation. The idealisation is not mere generalisation; even

when he was an intuitive image of it, the poet never leaves the concrete. Again, the theory maintains that the feelings alone can be raised to the state of aesthetic relish by the idealising capacity of poetry; but there is no adequate reason why the intuition of a descriptive matter, or even of a mere ornamental idea, cannot become an aesthetic fact. Just as the experience of feeling as feeling is not aesthetic intuition, so is also not the perception of matter or idea as such; they are only cases of the practical or logical forms of mental activity. But as soon as mere matter or idea, like mere feeling, becomes a part of the poetic intuition, it becomes a form of its spiritual activity, an aesthetic fact, capable of being equally relished. If the fertile dialectic acumen of Vāmana found the metaphorical in every aesthetic fact,* that of theorists like Viśvanātha found the sentimental in it. In laying stress upon sentimental poetry and distinguishing it from the descriptive or the ornamental, it falls back upon the old error of confusing the form with the essence. Nevertheless, the theory of *rasa* is a highly important and remarkable contribution. Sanskrit theorists were certainly aware of the aesthetic problem, but they did not attack it consistently in its entirety, contenting themselves in treating it only in some of its aspects.

2

THE PROBLEM

OF POETIC EXPRESSION

ONE OF THE fundamental problems of Sanskrit poetics, as indeed of all poetics, is the problem of the content and expression of poetry. From the beginning of the discipline, this was recognized.

The parts of language, the *śabda* and *artha** (word and sense), or, technically, the *vācaka* and *vācya*, (expressor and the expressed),* had already been distinguished by grammatical and philosophical speculation as the medium of linguistic expression. The essential element of all literature, as of all language, therefore, is said to consist of the material of word and sense, and the earliest definitions of poetry start in terms of *śabda* and *artha*. So long as poetry is a kind of expression, conveyed through the medium of language, this is inevitable.

Accordingly, Bhāmaha defines poetry as *śabdārthau sahitau kāvyam*. Subsequently, Rudrata's* more general statement refers to *śabdārthau kāvyam*, while Daṇḍin describes the body of poetry as *iṣṭārthavyavacchinnā padāvali*,* and Vāmana speaks of *viśiṣṭapadaracanā* as its essence. Thus, the *śabda* and *artha* united together, and not in themselves, constitute poetry, and all later writers more or less accept the position of the *sāhitya* (unity*) of *śabda* and *artha* as the starting point. The term sāhitya implies not only the unity of *śabda* and *artha*, but their inseparability as well. Kuntaka* describes this *sāhitya* as *anyūnānatiriktava** or *parasparaspardhā;** but Kālidāsa conveys it more beautifully by his well-known comparison of poetry to Ardhanārīśvara, in which Pārvatī is *vāc* or *śabda* and Parameśvara is *artha*.* That the poets, and not only the theorists, were aware of this idea is also clear from Māgha's declaration that the discerning poet pays equal regard to *śabda* and *artha* in the well-known line: *śabdārthau satkavir iva dvayaṃ vidvān apekṣate.*

This concept of the *sāhitya* of *śabda* and *artha*, from which literature itself came to take the designation of *sāhitya*, was not new. It had a grammatical origin, in which it meant the general grammatical and logical relation between word and sense in all linguistic expression. In this usage, the concept did not at first connote any special poetic relation between the two. As we noted earlier, Sanskrit poetics, like Sanskrit grammar, started as an empirical and normative discipline. From the very beginning, poetics accepted the authority of the older discipline of grammar, to which it was closely related. The grammatical speculations on speech in general not only prompted speculations on poetic speech, but also influenced their method and outlook. It is no wonder, then, that both Bhāmaha and Vāmana, two of the earliest formulators of poetic theory, devote whole sections of their works to the question of grammatical correctness; and the grammatical analysis of word and sense came to possess an important place in rhetorical speculation. As set forth by the grammarians, the *śabdārtha* or *vācakavācyasambandha* was taken to comprehend the consideration of the structure and variety of the *vācaka*, of the syntactic import of a succession of *vācakas* in a *vācya*, and of the logicality of the expressed idea; in other words, *pada,** *vākya,** and *pramāṇa** are comprehended in all expression and constituted the original meaning of *sāhitya.*

But it is also perceived that even though grammatical correctness or logical consistency characterises speech in general, this is not enough for poetic speech. What then is *sāhitya* from the standpoint of poetics? Bhāmaha's definition *śabdārthau sahitau kāvyam* implies that neither *śabda* nor *artha* alone is poetry, but both must be united together. In poetry there is no question of the superiority of the one or the other, or of the one being *bāhya* and the other *ābhyantara,** or, as Bhartṛhari puts it, of the *artha* being the *vivarta* of *śabda.* But mere *sāhitya* of *śabda* and *artha* is not poetry; it is a grammatical fact, common to all speech, to

the utterances of ordinary life, of *śāstra,** of *ākhyāna,** as well
as of poetry. It is realised, therefore, that this *sāhitya* of
poetry must be of a special kind, so that the special charm
of poetic speech, which distinguishes it from ordinary
speech, can be explained. *Śabda* and *artha* in their unity
bring about a special beauty in poetry which is not found
elsewhere; poetry is not merely linguistic expression, but
beautiful expression. In other words, it came to be recognised that the *sāhitya* of *śabda* and *artha* in poetry must
have a *viśeṣa* or specialty. Hence, Vāmana speaks of *viśiṣṭapadaracanā;* and Kuntaka declares more clearly that *viśiṣṭam
eva sāhityam abhipretam,* while Samudrabandha,* in sum-
marising the views of different schools of Poetics, is em-
phatic that *iha viśiṣṭau śabdārthau kāvyam.** The question
of deciding what this *viśeṣa* is and how it is realised thus
becomes the main problem of Poetics.

Some theorists approach the problem from the standpoint
of outward expression and declare the *viśeṣa* to be the
*dharma** of *śabda* and *artha,* which could be analysed into
categories of *lakṣaṇa,** *alaṃkāra,* or *guṇa.* Some dive deeper
into the content and maintain that it is the poet's peculiar
way, the work of his poetic imagination, the *kavivyāpāra,**
which is the *viśeṣa,* whether it takes the form of *ukti,
bhaṇiti, bhoga,* or *vyañjanā.** But it is admitted on all sides
that the *sāhitya,* which by its *viśeṣa* makes ordinary
śabdārtha into poetic *śabdārtha,* is not the sum total of
grammatical and logical relation, but indicates a certain
poetic relation between the two. It it the magical quality
pertaining to words and ideas, springing from the imaginative power of the poet, which makes ordinary utterance
with its *pada, vākya,* and *pramāṇa* into the charming utterance of poetry. The *sāhitya,* therefore, is a certain charming commensurateness between content and expression, and
becomes synonymous with poetry.

Exactly when and how the term *sāhitya* came to be employed for poetry in this technical sense we do not know,
but the concept is acknowledged from the very beginning.
It is no longer a grammatical, but a poetical, concept in
Rājaśekhara.* He mentions *sāhitya* and *sāhityavidyā* as

poetry and poetics, although in his allegorical description he does not bring out the theoretical implications of the idea. Among the theorists, the credit of divesting *sāhitya*, for the first time, of its original grammatical associations and defining it clearly as a poetic quality imparted by the imagination of the poet, belongs to Kuntaka.

Early speculations on the subject are vague and insufficient; several tentative approaches appear to have been made. One of the earliest was through the idea of *śayyā*,* to which Bāṇa refers, and for which the *Agnipurāṇa* appears to employ the term *mudrā** with a similar connotation. The *śayyā* is described as the repose of word and sense in their mutual favourableness, like the repose of the body in bed. The idea of *sāhitya* is also recognised in what is called the *maitrī* or mutual friendship of verbal and ideal elements of poetry, which is apparently a variation of Kālidāsa's more perfect conjugal metaphor. The theory is not elaborated, however, but only feebly and incoherently voiced here and there. Moreover, the *śayyā* is sometimes taken, strangely enough, as a mere verbal excellence; but, at the same time, it rightly insists upon what is called 'inevitability' of words and ideas as the foundation of poetic expression. The older views of *pāka*, mentioned by Vāmana, appear to make a similar approach, but greater uncertainty and confusion prevail. The term *pāka*, meaning literally ripeness or maturity, is employed by Vāmana with reference to the delightful effect of what he calls *śabdapāka* (maturity of words) resulting from what he considers to be the best mode of diction, the *Vaidarbhī rīti*.* He describes *śabdapāka* as that "attaining which the excellence of a word quickens and in which the unreal appears as real." This description would lead one to believe that Vāmana's *śabdapāka* is nothing more than mere verbal proficiency (*śabdavyutpatti*), in which sense some later writers would like to take the term.* But Vāmana further explains that the *śabdapāka* occurs when words are so chosen that they cannot bear an exchange of synonym. It is clear that this view makes *pāka* almost identical in its connotation with *śayyā*. And some later writers formulate *śabdapāka* as the perfect fitness of a word and its sense; but, in conformity with the prevailing view about the essentiality of *rasa*, they speak rather vaguely of *arthapāka* (maturity of sense) of various kinds brought about by the different state of different sentiments. In brief, then, the older views tended to formulate the theory of *pāka* as a variant of that of *śayyā*; but the theory takes such a wavering and uncertain direction in later times that it came to be regarded as a superfluous formality. When other and more convincing theories were advanced,* the *śayyā* and *pāka* almost disappear from Sanskrit poetic theories.

Bharata's concept of *lakṣaṇa** also belongs to the stage of uncertainty of early speculation which was groping to find a proper solution to the problem of *viśeṣa* or *viśiṣṭasāhitya* of *śabda* and *artha* as the basis of poetic expression. V. Raghavan has already given an exhaustive treatment of the history of this concept, and, since the *lakṣaṇapaddhati** perished very early, or lingered as a superfluous relic in the history of Sanskrit poetics and dramaturgy, it is not necessary for us to make more than a passing reference. Abhinavagupta, explaining Bharata's text, mentions as many as ten different views concerning *lakṣaṇa*; but it appears that *lakṣaṇa*, otherwise called *bhūṣaṇa,** is generally taken on the analogy of *sāmudrikalakṣaṇa,** to be an innate beautifying element belonging to the body of poetry, or rather constituting the body itself. Although similar in function to *alaṃkāra* in being a *kāvyaśobhākaradharma*, it is not a separate entity, but *apṛthaksiddha*; it imparts beauty to poetry by itself, and is not added, as an *alaṃkāra* is added, for extra beauty. It is obvious that the concept of *lakṣaṇa*, even at its birth, had an overlapping of functions with *alaṃkāra*, which in course of time swallowed it up. Even as a *nāṭakadharma,** connected with dramatic *saṃdhyaṅgas,** it had little individuality. The attitude of the *Daśarūpaka** in not considering it separately, but including it in *alaṃkāra* or *bhāva,** is significant. The main view, however, which takes *lakṣaṇa*, like *alaṃkāra*, as a beautifying characteristic, appears to have died out with Abhinavagupta's somewhat apologetic formulation. Nevertheless, the discussion furnishes interesting evidence of an early tentative attempt to explain the essential character of poetic expression.

This brings us to the first systematic approach to the problem, made by the so-called *alaṃkāra* school of Bhāmaha, Udbhaṭa, and Rudraṭa, from which starts the earliest known formulation of a definite theory of poetic expression. Although as a theory of expression the *ālaṃkārika** view was subsequently discarded for its insufficiency, the concept of *alaṃkāra* persisted and its utility was acknowledged throughout the history of Sanskrit poetics. It is, therefore, important to consider and understand the concept of *alaṃkāra*, in its various aspects, as the *viśeṣa* or specialty of the *śabda* and *artha*.

What then is *alaṃkāra?* To this fundamental question, neither Bhāmaha, Udbhaṭa, nor Rudraṭa furnishes a precise answer. From their treatment it appears that the term *connotes* an extraordinary turn given to ordinary expression, which makes ordinary speech (ordinary *śabdārthasāhitya*) into poetic speech (poetic *śabdārthasāhitya*), and *denotes* the entire assemblage of rhetorical ornaments as means of poetic expression. In other words, *alaṃkāra* connotes the underlying principle of expression and denotes its means of realisation; the term indicates embellishment itself as well as the means of embellishment. In later poetics, *alaṃkāra* is almost exclusively restricted to its denotation of poetic figures as means of embellishment, and in this sense it is also known to Bharata and Bhāmaha; but its connotation as the principle of embellishment appears in a somewhat fluid state in the early works of Bhāmaha, Daṇḍin and Vāmana.*

To the individual poetic figures (like simile or metaphor), the prominence of which is palpable in his system, Bhāmaha applies the term *alaṃkāra;* but he also employs the term *vakrokti* as a collective designation of such individual poetic figures. *Vakrokti*, however, is not used as synonymous with *alaṃkāra*. As a collective designation, the former doubtless denotes the poetic figures as such, but it also connotes a deviating strikingness of expression which underlies all individual poetic figures and forms their distinguishing characteristic. It is, thus, the fundamental principle of figurative expression; but since Bhāmaha regards figurative expression to be the only proper expression of poetry, the *vakrokti* becomes the distinguishing characteristic of poetic expression and the essential principle of poetry itself.

Bhāmaha does not define *vakrokti*. Like the term *alaṃkāra*, it was perhaps already traditionally established. But in speaking of it in connexion with the figure *atiśayokti*, he perhaps implies in it the *lokātikrāntagocaraṃ vacaḥ,** which he expressly mentions as a characteristic of *atiśayokti*. As explained by Abhinavagupta and developed by Kuntaka, the qualification perhaps implies a heightened form of expression, an imaginative quality which constitutes a poetic figure, and as such distinguishes poetic speech from the matter-of-fact speech of everyday life. All poetic expression involves some kind of expressional deviation which constitutes its charm. Bhāmaha's *vakrokti* signifies this expressional deviation proper to poetry. Examining the whole field of poetic expression, Bhāmaha finds the *alaṃkāra* or poetic figure omnipresent as a means of realising this deviation, and *vakrokti* becomes the essential principle of an *alaṃkāra*, and necessarily of poetry itself.

Although Daṇḍin uses the term *vakrokti* only once in a significant passage as a collective designation of individual *alaṃkāras*, and thus far agrees with Bhāmaha, he does not apply it to the essential poetic quality underlying an individual *alaṃkāra*. On the other hand, he applies the term *alaṃkāra* itself generically to the attribute, apparently of word and sense, which produces beauty in poetry, the *kāvyaśobhākaradharma* of *śabda* and *artha*. Even though he does not define *kāvyaśobhā* (poetic beauty), he agrees with Bhāmaha that the entire *vāṇmaya** (poetic speech) is comprehended by *vakrokti* (figurative expression), with only the exception of the first or primary figure, the so-called *svabhāvokti* (natural description). The reservation made with regard to *svabhāvokti* is not found in Bhāmaha. But it cannot be said that, like Kuntaka, Bhāmaha entirely rejects the figure; he mentions it with the guarded remark *iti kecit pracakṣate.* In so far as natural description involves strikingness of expression, it would be admissible, but Bhāmaha would not then consider it separately; it would be included in the scope of his *vakrokti* as figurative expression.

Although Daṇḍin would employ the term *alaṃkāra* as the essential poetic attribute of *śabda* and *artha* and the beautifying principle of poetic expression, he would not take the individual *alaṃkāras* as the sole or essential means of the beautifying principle. He elaborates a theory of two modes (*mārga**) or kinds of poetic diction, which he calls Vaidarbha and Gauḍa,* and finds that the so-called excellences (*guṇas*, like sweetness or lucidity) form their essence.* Daṇḍin, therefore, employs the generic term *alaṃkāra*, meaning poetic embellishment, to designate both the *guṇas*, on the one hand, and the specific *alaṃkāras* (poetic figures), on the other.

The concept of *guṇa* is not new, having been mentioned by Bharata, but it is considered in a new context. It is, however, neither properly defined, nor its relation to the old concept of *alaṃkāra* exactly determined. Daṇḍin tells us only that the *guṇa* is an *alaṃkāra* belonging to the *Vaidarbhamārga* exclusively, while the poetic figure is an *alaṃkāra* which is common to both the *mārgas*. Thus, it appears that the *guṇa*, in his opinion, forms the essence or essential condition of what he considers to be the best poetic diction, but *alaṃkāra* as poetic figure, on which the *alaṃkāra* school of Bhāmaha laid exclusive stress, is not the special characteristic of any specific diction, for it may reside in all kinds of diction. Every *guṇa*, according to Daṇḍin, is an *alaṃkāra*, but he states nowhere that every specific *alaṃkāra* is a *guṇa*.

Vāmana further develops the rather indefinite ideas of Daṇḍin regarding *alaṃkāra* and *guṇa*. He follows Daṇḍin in taking *alaṃkāra* both in its denotation and connotation, but he draws a more rigid line of distinction between *guṇa* and *alaṃkāra*. He states at the outset that poetry is acceptable on account of *alaṃkāra*, and he is careful to explain that the term should be taken here not in the specific sense of poetic figure but in the general sense of poetic beauty. He, therefore, lays down sententiously that *alaṃkāra* is beauty (*saundaryam alaṃkāraḥ*). He also explains that the term *alaṃkāra* is primarily synonymous with the act of embellishing, but in a secondary, instrumental sense it is applied to that which embellishes or to the means of embellishment. In all this he is evidently developing Daṇḍin's teaching; and like Daṇḍin, but more clearly, he does not make the presence of poetic figures, like simile and metaphor, an essential condition or requisite, as he does with respect to the presence of *guṇas*. The *guṇa* is defined as an essential characteristic of *rīti*, which term Vāmana employs for Daṇḍin's *mārga*. The *rīti* being, in his opinion, the essence of poetry, the *guṇas* are those characteristics which create the beauty of poetry, *kāvyaśobhāyāḥ kartāro dharmāḥ*, a function which is assigned by Daṇḍin to both the *guṇas* and the so-called *alaṃkāras* (poetic figures). The *alaṃkāras*, in his opinion, are such means of embellishment as serve to heighten the beauty created by the *guṇas*, *tadatiśayahetavaḥ*. The *guṇa*, therefore, being the *sine qua non* of poetic expression, is described as *nitya*,[*] implying that the *alaṃkāra* is *anitya*; the *guṇa* is the *dharma* of *rīti*, which is the 'soul' (*ātman*) of poetry, while the *alaṃkāra* is apparently the *dharma* of *śabda* and *artha*, which constitute its body.[*] In other words, the *alaṃkāra* without the *guṇa* cannot by itself produce the beauty of poetry, which the *guṇa* can do without the *alaṃkāra*. Although Vāmana declares at the outset that the term poetry applies to such word and sense as are beautified by *guṇa* and *alaṃkāra* (*kāvyaśabdo 'yam guṇālaṃkṛtayoḥ śabdārthayor vartate*), yet the *guṇa*, which is rigidly differentiated from *alaṃkāra*, is taken as the essence of poetic expression in his system.

Vāmana, like Bhāmaha and Daṇḍin, acknowledges the omnipresence and utility of *alaṃkāra* as a means of poetic expression; he also elaborates, after Daṇḍin, a theory of *rīti-guṇa* to explain the *viśeṣa*[*] of *śabdārthasāhitya*. He defines *rīti* as particular arrangement of words (*viśiṣṭapada-racanā*), and explains the *viśeṣa* (particularity of arrangement) as consisting of the *guṇa*, realised in varying degrees in various kinds of *rīti*. Whether the idea of *rīti*, like that of *pravṛtti* of Bharata,* was evolved from geographical association and named *Vaidarbhī*, *Gauḍī*, and *Pāñcālī* accordingly, but was afterwards standardised with reference to the subject, it is clear that in Vāmana's system it is synonymous with the literary mode displayed in various distinguishable types of poetic diction, realised by the unification of certain well-defined 'excellences', such as sweetness and lucidity, which are called *guṇas*. The *alaṃkāras* (like simile and metaphor), on the other hand, are, no doubt, means of poetic expression; but they are merely striking turns of word and sense which have a subsidiary value.

From this brief review of the growth of the fundamental concepts of *alaṃkāra* and *guṇa-rīti*, it is clear that, both the *alaṃkāra* and *rīti* Schools start with *śabda* and *artha*, word and sense, and find their *sāhitya* to consist of the poetic *viśeṣa* of *alaṃkāra* and *guṇa-rīti* as the essential *dharma* of *śabda* and *artha* respectively. While these early theories rightly call attention to an extraordinary quality in the relation of word and sense in poetic expression which distinguishes it from ordinary expression, their inadequacy from the aesthetic point of view is evident. Their acute analysis of outward form and technique, with which they mainly concern themselves, is admirable, but they forget that the explanation of mere verbal and ideational arrangement is not sufficient for explaining the fact of poetic expression. Mere enumeration of categories of rhetorical embellishment or of so-called literary excellences does not adequately explain why they embellish or why they are excellent. As the *dhvani* theorists rightly criticise, these earlier views do not correlate outward poetic expression to the inner content of poetry; nor do they, as Kuntaka rightly points out, correlate poetic expression to the individuality of the poet, to the *kavisvabhāva*.

While the *alaṃkāra* school employs the term *alaṃkāra* to connote the fundamental characteristic or principle of the beauty of poetic expression, in actual theory and practice it is applied to the objective beauty of poetic form realised by certain decorative devices known as poetic figures. Poetic expression, in this view, is chiefly figurative or rhetorical expression. Even if Bhāmaha speaks of *vakrokti* as an essential principle of poetic expression, he does not define it nor does he elaborate the idea in all its implication. His successors Udbhaṭa and Rudraṭa neither mention the term nor discuss the principle. The attempts of these exponents of the *alaṃkāra* school are limited, as we noted previously, to systematic classification of poetic expression into fixed rhetorical categories. This formal treatment affords their works the general appearance of technical manuals comprising a collection of definitions, illustrations, and empirical canons elaborated for the benefit of the aspiring poet. Poetry is regarded, more or less, as a mechanical series of verbal devices. A desirable sense must prevail, diversified by means of various tricks of phrasing* (to which the name *alaṃkāra* is restricted) consisting of the so-called poetic figures.

These theorists approach expression and embellishment as a positive or accomplished fact to be methodically collected in their greatest possible variety, analysed with acute scholastic acumen, and grouped in fixed classes and types. In other words, they devote their effort chiefly to working out into an exact system the rules and means, formulas and categories, of external production. This practical or pedagogic outlook must have received great impetus from the highly developed analytic enquiry into the forms of language made by the normative grammarians. Like the grammarian and the scientist, who label and classify ever new series of facts, the Sanskrit *ālaṃkārika*,* pretending to find universals, calculates the particular species of expression from the original four 'ornaments' of Bharata* to the one hundred and twenty-five of Appayya Dīkṣita;* but considering the inexhaustibility of individual poetic expression, the ornaments may be easily renewed to an infinite number, while the 'universals' of a formal analysis are of doubtful theoretic value for explaining the principle of concrete individual expression itself.

The aesthetic insufficiency of rhetorical categories was speedily perceived. But the theories which were advanced against mere rhetoric did not entirely reject it. On the contrary, a reserve was made regarding its utility, and its principles were carefully preserved. When Vāmana declared the essence of poetic expression to be the *rīti*, by which he meant nothing but a specific arrangement of words, characterised by the 'qualities' or *guṇas*, he did not advance the speculation much further; nor did his predecessor Daṇḍin, to whom poetry was nothing more than a series of words determined by a desired sense. Both agree that the words should have a *vyavacchinna, viśiṣṭa,* or particular arrangement,* but this *viśeṣa* consists not only of a special disposition (*rīti*) but also of ornamentation (*alaṃkāra*). Daṇḍin gives an extended interpretation of the term 'ornament', applying it to anything which lends 'beauty' (*śobhā*) to poetry, and including in its scope the figurative devices as well as modes or grades of arrangement of word and sense.* Vāmana substantially agrees with this view when he defines 'ornament' as beauty itself; but with regard to the means of realising this beauty he draws a sharp distinction between particularities of arrangement and the mere figures of poetic speech, viewing them as essential and accidental means respectively.

It must, however, be made clear that the term 'beauty' (*śobhā* or *saundarya*), which is taken as the test of poetic expression, is not clearly defined. There is no exposition of its character, even if its means are described and detailed. But the concept appears to refer to the logical external effect realised by a carefully worked out adjustment of word and sense, which avoids damaging flaws by adopting, primarily, the so-called literary 'qualities', and secondarily, the rhetorical figures for heightening the effect thus produced. Whatever attempt later theorists like Kuntaka might have made to place the concept on a better aesthetic footing, or in whatever sense later writers might have employed it, there can be no doubt that the term *rīti* in Daṇḍin and Vāmana signified nothing more nor less than a specific arrangement of word and sense, a mere combination, in varying degrees, of clearly defined 'qualities' like 'perspicuity' or 'smoothness', and incidentally of equally clearly defined rhetorical figures like simile or metaphor. It has no reference to the organic expressive activity of the poetic intuition, which Kuntaka calls *kavivyāpāra*, nor is it made equivalent, in this sense, to the Western concept of 'style' as the expression of poetic individuality. The *rīti*, as understood by these early theorists, is capable of technical formulation. Thus the 'qualities' like 'simplicity', 'vivacity', and so forth, become only generic or specific categories for labelling particular aspects of the aesthetic activity; they do not explain the true character of the activity itself. *Rīti* and its constituent 'qualities' properly designate the different degrees in the development, free or less free, of the expressive activity, and are thus aspects of successful or less successful expression. When completely successful, we have the expression itself. The so-called *doṣas** (flaws) designate embarrassed activity, ending in failure, and are thus aspects of unsuccessful expression.

From the aesthetic point of view, this success or failure of expression may also be termed beauty or ugliness. But the beautiful, as the perfect expression, does not possess degrees; if ugliness does, complete ugliness, as complete negation, altogether ceases to be ugly—it loses its contradiction, and is no longer an aesthetic fact. The consideration of expression itself, therefore, is important, not the scholastic definition and classification of its different degrees of success or failure, of freedom or bondage.

The distinction, again, which the *rīti*-theorists draw between *guṇa* and *alaṃkāra* lacks a proper aesthetic foundation. They find that both impart 'beauty' to poetry; that is, both are parts or means of perfect expression. Some, like Daṇḍin, say that there is little difference between the two as means of producing beauty, the one being a generic and the other a specific term. Others* feel that they differ but slightly, the *guṇa* being the *dharma* of the collocation of word and sense as a whole, and *alaṃkāra*, of *śadba* and *artha*. The view was also proposed that the *guṇa* was *śobhāhetu*, and *nitya*, while the *alaṃkāra* was useful for 'extra beauty', *śobhātiśayahetu*, and *anitya*.

All these theorists realised only that both *guṇa* and *alaṃkāra* impart beauty. They did not understand the vital question: To what in poetry do they impart beauty? They failed to perceive that *guṇa* and *alaṃkāra*, in whatever sense they are used, are only relative terms, and that they imply a *guṇin* and *alaṃkārya*.* Vāmana, no doubt, stumbled upon something more than *guṇa* and *alaṃkāra*, upon what he calls *rīti*; but, Ānandavardhana rightly points out, the *rīti* theorists thereby only dimly perceived the nature of the essence of poetry, which cannot be the mere objective beauty realised by *rīti-guṇa* and *alaṃkāra*. The distinction between literary qualities and rhetorical 'ornaments' as essential and nonessential may be of some use in logical or normative analysis, but not in aesthetic realisation. Given a particular expression, the 'qualities' are as much integral parts of it as figures of speech. The expression should be taken not as a mechanic, but as an organic, whole in relation to the poetic intuition. As each individual expression automatically selects its own appropriate 'qualities' and 'ornaments', it cannot be definitely laid down that a particular expression should possess this and should not possess that. If expression is expression, it is succesful; there cannot be any question of intermediate degrees of success in aesthetic estimate. Kuntaka, therefore, rightly criticises that there can be no classification of *rīti* into good, bad, or indifferent types. Nor can qualities or ornaments be categorically attached, for such expression is not a fixed and generic, but a variable and individual fact. Kuntaka appropriately observes that the concepts of *rīti*, *guṇa* and *alaṃkāra* can be justified only if they are related to the *kavikarman* or *kavisvabhāva*, to the imagination or individuality of particular poets.

Poetic expression is capable of infinite diversity in accordance with the infinite diversity of poetic individuality. Daṇḍin wisely declares that speech is diversified in its multifarious modes of expression and admits the impossibility of labelling and classifying all modes of poetic expression with fixed and unalterable characteristics. But, while maintaining that the subvarieties are incalculable, he distinguishes two broad or extreme types, *Vaidarbhī* and *Gaudī*. His successor Vāmana proposes three types, adding *Pāñcālī* as intermediate, and recommending the *Vaidarbhī* as containing all the 'qualities'. Subsequent writers add *Lāṭī, Āvantikā, Māgadhī,* and so forth.*

The attempt to exhaust and stereotype the entire poetical output within the clear-cut bounds of ready-made modes and fixed 'qualities' on the basis of more-or-less formal analysis, like the similar attempt of the *alaṃkāra* school to classify and label the entire poetic expression into fixed rhetorical categories, is sure to prove unconvincing as a theoretic basis of poetic expression. Neither Daṇḍin's nor Vāmana's differentiation of individual *rītis* and *guṇas,* is, as the criticism of Mammaṭa and others shows, exhaustive and consistent.* These varieties of *rīti,* with their constituent *guṇas,* are really instances of complete and incomplete expression erected into purportedly universal types, probably (as the names imply) on the basis of empirical observation of localised usages. But, as Kuntaka shows, the *rīti* cannot be a *deśadharma* as localised usage, nor a *vastudharma* as an inherent attribute of word and sense; it is a *dharma* of *kavisvabhāva* (the character of the poet) depending upon the nature of his poetic intuition, upon his *śakti* (poetic power), *vyutpatti* (culture), and *abhyāsa* (practice).

In this sense the *rīti* becomes synonymous with the manner of individual poets, and not with prescribed or universalised modes or grades, and all aspects of expression can be comprehended in it. But since the manner of expression varies with various poets, it is of infinite kind. It can be classified under broad types, but the definition and classification are susceptible to infinite, but unprofitable, multiplication.

3

THE POETIC IMAGINATION

WITH THE STANDARDISATION of the scheme of poetics outlined by the *rasa-dhavani* theorists, which we have described,* it was thought that there was nothing new to set forth. Subsequently, the history of Sanskrit poetics, with one or two notable exceptions presents hardly any new idea of theoretic importance or any fresh effort to reexamine fundamental problems. There was necessarily a falling back upon matters of detail for the purpose of explanation, expansion, differentiation, or restriction of already established ideas, norms, and categories, which helped to satisfy the growing scholastic passion for hair-splitting distinctions and the dialectic bent for controversy over verbal formalism.

Thus, one finds in the works of this later stage a great deal of elaborative acumen expressed in the same stock manner and phraseology, but very little originality or understanding of aesthetic facts. Some writers are excellent analysts of minutiae. Others are frankly unsystematic or merely eclectic. A very large number of them hold to the modest ambition of producing nothing more than a popular textbook on conventional lines. They are fine reasoners rather than contemplators of artistic creation. Some attempt to arrive at a rigorous definition of poetry, a task wisely left alone by the previous thinkers; but, in their zeal to find a comprehensive logical formula, they touch only the externals, forget all about the creative imagination, and wind up in hopeless inconsistencies. The fecundity of their attempts is seen in the empirical collection of single facts; but infecundity is revealed by their perplexity over exhausting the ever renewed multiplication of single facts, by their uncertainty in pointing indefinitely to this and this and this fact as art. It was an age of commentaries and of commentaries on commentaries. The dogmas and formulas persisted, and the study began more and more to revert back to its original normative character.

Rhetoric was still there for those who were unable to assimilate any other kind of nourishment. But, brushing aside all this uninspiring scholastic verbalism and formalism, we can still find here and there some scattered glimpses of theoretic speculation, mostly in the heretics and minor writers rather than in the major orthodox personages. Bhaṭṭa Nāyaka,* for instance, whose work unfortunately is lost, appears to have altogether denied the unexpressed of the *dhvani* theorists as an essential of poetic creation, regarding it only as an accidental element or aspect of expression. Kuntaka, whose work has been recovered partially, attempted to give a new turn to the speculation by his endeavour to rethink the subject and arrange it differently. He is one of the very few writers who took into consideration, however imperfectly, the creative imagination of the poet.*

Kuntaka attempts to develop further the idea of *vakrokti** vaguely present in Bhāmaha, and systematises the views of those who stressed figures of speech as the essential feature of poetry. But in the course of his investigation he appears to have stumbled upon certain poetic principles which go beyond the sphere of his formal analysis. By *vakrokti,* which Kuntaka considers essential in poetic expression, he apparently thinks chiefly of figurative forms of speech, for which he often uses the phrase as a collective name;* but, as we shall see presently, this is not for him the entire significance of the term. Poetry to him is nothing but embellished sound and sense, the embellishment being chiefly (but not exclusively*) figurative device. And, as this is the only ornament (*alaṃkāra*) possible and essential, he rejects the views of those who omit figurative expressions from consideration or regard them as accidental or nonessential. The skill of the poet,* in his opinion, can and does exhibit the forms of *vakrokti* in the arrangement of letters, in the base or termination of words, in a sentence, in a particular topic, or in the composition as a whole. While all this may be formal analysis in the service of logic and rhetoric, Kuntaka in his conception of the fundamentals of *vakrokti* itself shows himself cognisant of the aesthetic problem, even if he does not deal with it clearly and completely.

He well understood that art could not be made the medium of philosophical, religious, or scientific concepts, and insisted upon a clear distinction between *śāstra* and *kāvya*, between intellective and imaginative work, stating that the words and ideas of the *kāvya* differ from the words and ideas of the *śāstra*. He also maintains that poetic speech is an extraordinary deviation from the ordinary mode of common speech, thereby distinguishing artistic expression from what he considers to be the merely naturalistic. This extraordinariness (*vakratva* or *vakrabhāva*) depends upon an imaginative turn of words and ideas, which he calls *bhaṅgībhaṇiti,** peculiar to poetic expression and abhorrent of logical or matter-of-fact expression. He further explains that *bhaṅgībhaṇiti* or *vakratva*, for which another word is *vaicitrya* or *vicchitti* (strikingness or charmingness), is the expression of the *vidagdha*, the man versed in belles lettres, who must be distinguished from the *vidvat*, the mere scholar. He further explains that this expression rests upon the intuition (*pratibhā*) of the poet, or on his skill (*kauśala*), or on an act of imagination on his part, which is termed *kavivyāpāra* or *kavikarman* (poetic function), but which is not defined or explained.

It is obvious that Kuntaka is one of the few Sanskrit theorists who puts a clear emphasis on the imaginative power of the poet and considers it to be the source of the characteristic charm of poetic expression. He regards embellished speech as poetry, but holds that the source of this embellishment, even if it consists of figures of speech, is the poetic imagination. He therefore draws a distinction between what may be called speech figure, on the one hand, and poetic figure on the other. In a formal scheme of poetics they may correspond. But in a poetic figure Kuntaka discovers a differentia which consists of a peculiar turn of expression (*vakratva*) resulting in a characteristic strikingness (*vicchitti* or *vaicitrya*) and depends on the imaginative activity of the poet (*kavipratibhānirvartitatva*). The so-called figures of orthodox poetics are admissible only when they possess these characteristics of peculiar charm imparted by the imagination of the poet, the word 'charm' apparently meaning nothing but that which gives the expression its poetic peculiarity. Kuntaka maintains, therefore, that embellishments do not 'belong' to poetry; that is to say, they are not added externally, but poetry is embellished speech itself, the particular embellishment depending on the poetic imagination.

Kuntaka thus supplies a deficiency in the teaching of the *rasa-dhvani* theorists who, ignoring poetic imagination, did not consider it worthwhile to take the embellishments at all into serious account. To them the ornamental expression of poetry was a detachable, external, and nonessential addition. Kuntaka gave a new interpretation and justification of the poetic figures. If they are a part of the poetic expression, they have a right to be considered, for they form the expression itself. The question of essentiality or nonessentiality does not arise. Since, in Kuntaka's view, poetry is always embellished expression, as distinguished from the plain and matter-of-fact expression of science and scriptures, embellishment in the general sense is always a characteristic of poetic expression. This embellishment comprehends in its specific sense the whole domain of rhetorical figures, if they are justified by the poetic imagination and become poetic figures thereby. It may also include the 'qualities', as well as feelings, mere matter, or the so-called unexpressed, if as form or material these too are a part of the poetic intuition and expression. Thus, he gives an extended interpretation to Bhāmaha's *vakrokti*, by which Kuntaka connotes and denotes the same thing, namely, the heightened form of imaginative expression. He makes Bhāmaha's vague connotation of mere hyperbolic speech more definite by referring it to the poetic imagination. It is, therefore, inaccurate to suppose that Kuntaka accepts merely figurative expression as the denotation of *vakrokti*, for he brings within its comprehensive scope all known kinds of imaginative expression. The inaccuracy arises from the apparent emphasis he puts on figurative expression for justifying it in poetry, but in reality his *vakrokti* is much more than that.

It is a pity that this explanation of poetic expression and imagination was never seriously noticed nor fully developed by orthodox writers, for it might have led ultimately to a clear idea of the nature of poetic creation, an aspect of the question which was ignored by Sanskrit theorists. But later writers, even if they neglected Kuntaka's work and let it fall into unmerited oblivion, appear to have accepted, directly or implicitly, his idea of a poetic figure and applied his test of poetic imagination, albeit only piecemeal, to their own analyses of rhetorical categories. Ruyyaka,* for instance, takes the charm brought about by the productive imagination of the poet to be the criterion of a poetic figure. Thus, he thinks that a form of expression involving the logical *anumāna** would not *prima facie* constitute the figure *anumāna*, unless it involved this poetic charm; or, the doubt involved in the figure *saṃdeha** must be brought into being by the imagination of the poet, for it should not be an ordinary doubt but a 'poetic' doubt. In these and similar cases the question is not one of a mere form of speech, in which nothing is given but the bare thought; it must be the expression of the poetic imagination. Jayaratha, who has commented upon Ruyyaka's treatise, informs us that it is not possible to define this poetic charm (*vicchitti*), inasmuch as it is of infinite variety, identical with the play of the poetic imagination which is itself infinite in scope. The infinite individuations of the poetic imagination had already been admitted by Ānandavardhana as well as by Kuntaka. Jagannātha, however, attempts a general definition, saying that this charm is nothing but the poetic imagination with reference to the power of poetic production.

These speculations are of no little value in calling attention to the creative imagination, which Kuntaka may be said to have 'discovered'. If Ānandavardhana explained the poetic intuition in the *sāmājika** with respect to the aesthetic enjoyment of poetic creations, he left out of consideration the question of the poetic intuition with reference to the poet himself. In other words, he had considered the reader's power of reproduction, but not the poet's power of production. Kuntaka for the first time raised the issue, maintaining that we should start with the creative imagination of the poet himself, of which poetic expression or creation is the actuality. If he had resolutely pursued his investigations further on this line, he might have formulated a proper aesthetic; but he still shows himself a victim of rhetorical and other categories in a different form. The scholastic tendency was almost universal and proved too difficult a bar for Kuntaka to surmount completely. While he discovered the poetic imagination, he cannot have the credit of developing its implication for the entire aesthetic question. He applied it chiefly to the analysis of figurative and cognative expression.

He had an inkling of truth when he spoke of poetic speech as a kind of proposition other than that represented by scientific or popular speech. In making the distinction he spoke indeed of the poetic imagination, but he could not clearly see that, inasmuch as the intellective and the intuitive are both aspects of the spiritual activity, the distinction is not absolute; it depends simply on the nature of the poetic intuition. There is thus no absolute distinction aesthetically between the simple and the ornate, for both may equally well become kinds of poetic expression—or, better, the expression itself. A scientific work can very well become a work of art if the writer has a poetic intuition of scientific facts and converts them into intuitive facts. Kuntaka's discussions on the figure *svabhāvokti* (natural description),* as well as his main preoccupation with figurative expression, indicate that he could not get himself entirely out of the conventional groove. The distinction was to him, in practice, an empirical distinction between the simple and the ornate, and led him to put greater emphasis on ornamental expression. His *vakrokti* degenerates into the mere *kaviprauḍhokti** of later writers. He started well on his journey of discovery, but stood halfway, enmeshed and uncertain. If he perceived a serious flaw in the conventional edifice, he never ventured to take the giant's step of giving it the final blow.

The next interesting writer, Rājaśekhara,* was, in spite of his pretensions, neither a poet nor a heretic. He has given us no systematic theory, but a curious jumble of disjointed thoughts and suggestions in his high-sounding *Kāvya-mīmāṃsā* (*Enquiry into Poetry*). Yet, he was aware, however vaguely, of the function of the poetic imagination.

It is difficult to evaluate Rājaśekhara, however, for it is futile to seek in this work of his for any consistent idea. For instance, he declares that bad poetry is like living death, but it cannot be said that he could very clearly distinguish between science and poetry, between *śāstra* and *kāvya*.* It is not surprising that he gives an inconclusive classification of two kinds of poets, the *śāstrakavi* (who may either compose the *śāstra* or produce *kāvya* effect in the *śāstra* or *śātra* effect in the *kāvya*) and the *kāvyakavi*. In other words, he thinks that the poetic imagination can produce a scientific work as well as a poem, or combine both, as such, in varying proportions! To be sure, poetry and science may meet on the aesthetic side; as we have remarked, the intellective and the intuitive are merely aspects of the spiritual activity. But when the activity of the intellect passes into that of the imagination the scientific work becomes a work of art.

More fortunate, however, are Rājaśekhara's remarks on *pratibhā* (poetic imagination). The *pratibhā*, in his opinion, is the power of the poet which illuminates; the illumination is inward (for a blind man also can be a poet) and enables the poet to conceive even unseen and far-off things. He holds further that the *pratibhā* may have a twofold aspect, according as it is creative (*kārayitrī*) or discriminative (*bhāvayitrī**), the former serving the poet and the latter helping the appreciator of the poet's production. Haphazard and uncertain as these observations are, they are still interesting glimpses of truth dimly discerned.

The rationalistic theorists are less inspiring. Mahimabhaṭṭa,* who affords a curious example of this group, pushes the grammatico-logical attitude to its extreme form. He thinks that poetry is as much the medium of the facts of logic or of thought as science, and that all poetic expression is reducible to the syllogistic form. If by this opinion he understands the aesthetic principle of coherent expression, his contention is legitimate; for, having a clear intuition of one's own thought, one will necessarily express it logically and well. But since Mahimabhaṭṭa attempts to prove syllogistically the facts of poetic intuition, which are not universal but individual facts, we can dismiss his view as insufficient for the explanation of poetic expression.

Kṣemendra,* on the other hand, does not concern himself directly with the question of poetic imagination, but takes as his thesis the theory of *aucitya* (propriety) already discussed by Ānandavardhana.* He is undoubtedly right in developing the view that proper expression is the only expression, in fact, it is expression itself; but his investigations are directed mainly to the consideration of externals. Accepting the prevailing view that the suggestion of *rasa* alone is essential in poetry, he analyses the improprieties which hinder this aesthetic enjoyment. Accordingly, he distinguishes and classifies minutely, with profuse illustrations, the applications of the principle of propriety to the various points in a poem, such as a word, a sentence, the subject-matter, the speaker, the time and place, the qualities, the poetic figures, the underlying sentiment, the employment of the verb, preposition, adjectives, and particles, the use of case, number, and gender, and so forth. He dogmatically summarises the cases of application as twenty-seven in number. All this is very useful; but it forgets that the infinite variations of individual poetic expression are incapable of exhaustive formal treatment, and that nothing is gained by tabulating generically certain forms or aspects of an ever-changing spiritual activity.

Nevertheless, Kṣemendra, who was perhaps a better critic than a poet, displays in most cases a great deal of insight in his criticism, and does not always confine himself to rigid rules and specific definitions. He takes even Kālidāsa to task, against the authority of Ānandavardhana, for the vulgarity of canto VIII of the *Kumārasaṃbhava,* which he considers improper to the particular conception of his great poem. And, as an instance of detail, one may cite Kṣemendra's accute criticism of Kālidāsa's use in the same work of the colourless word *bhāva* as a designation of Rudra, the terrible god of destruction; for he thinks that it mars the mighty effect of the few swift words describing the tragic annihilation of Madana, the love god.* Kṣemendra's small work in this respect possesses a unique value, giving evidence of taste and critical judgement, which are comparatively rare or only incidental in Sanskrit.

Very closely connected with the theory of propriety (*aucitya*) is the much older idea of *śayyā* and *pāka** which is feebly and incoherently voiced here and there by some of the minor personages. But, vaguely and only incidentally considered as it is, the theory rightly focuses upon what is popularity called 'felicity of expression', holding that the expression depends upon the poetic imagination and that 'felicity of expression' means nothing more than the perfect expression of a poetic intuition, which is, simply, its only expression. For every aesthetic fact exist only its appropriate words; every other kind of words is improper. Bāṇa has already used the word *śayyā,** and the *Agnipurāṇa* employs the word *mudrā* with a similar connotation.* It is defined as the repose of word and sense in mutual favourableness, like the repose of the body in a bed, the similitude explaining the etymology of the term. This *maitrī* (mutual friendship of verbal and ideal elements of poetry) is held to be so close that the words cannot be replaced by synonyms. It is thus a theory of the inevitability of words, claiming that each poetic intuition has its appropriate and unalterable word counterpart, and which, forming the very foundation of artistic expression, distinguishes at once the conceptual language of science from the intuitive language of poetry. But the Sanskrit theorists never went so far; they spoke of *śayyā* merely as a special verbal excellence without developing its aesthetic implications for a theory of expression.

Greater uncertainty and confusion are seen in the closely allied views on *pāka*. The term *pāka*, meaning literally ripeness or maturity, is as old as Vāmana,* who speaks of the delightful effect of the maturity of words (*śabdapāka*) resulting from what he considers to be the best mode of diction (*Vaidarbhī rīti*). He describes it as "that attaining which the excellence of a word quickens and in which the unreal appears as real." He explains again that the *śabdapāka* occurs when the words are so chosen that they cannot bear an exchange of synonym. This view makes *pāka* identical in its connotation with *śayyā*. Following Vāmana, a few later writers formulate *śabdapāka* as the perfect fitness of word and its sense; but in conformity with the prevailing view about the essentiality of *rasa*, they speak rather vaguely of *arthapāka* (maturity of sense) as depth of sense of various kinds brought about by the different tastes of different poetic sentiments.* Others, again, think of maturity of words as mere verbal proficiency (*śabdavyupatti*).

Rājaśekhara's* naïve compilation of earlier views on the subject is interesting and deserves reference, for it illustrates how undecided the aesthetic opinions were, and how inconstant the use of aesthetic terminology:

The *Ācāryas** ask: "What is *pāka?*" Mangala* says: "It is maturity [*pariṇāma*]." "What, again, is maturity?" ask the *Ācāryas*. Mangala replies: "It is verbal excellence [*sauśabdya*]." "The *pāka* is fixedness in the application of words" say the *Ācāryas*. It is said [by Vāmana]: "The insertion and deletion of words occur so long as there is uncertainty in the mind; when the fixity of words is established, the composition is successful." So the followers of Vāmana say: "The *pāka* is the aversion of words to alteration by means of synonyms." Therefore it is said: "The specialists in the propriety of words have called that *śabdapāka* in which the words abandon the capability of being exchanged [by synonyms]."

Despite the quaintness of this somewhat rambling discourse, it is clear that the older views tended to formulate the theory of *pāka* as a variant of that of *śayyā;* but the theory takes such a wavering and uncertain direction in later conventional theorists, who betray a tendency to regard it, more or less, as a superfluous formality, that in the end the theory entirely disappears from Sanskrit poetics. Rājaśekhara continues:

But Avantisundarī* thinks that this want of capability [of words for being replaced by synonyms] is not *pāka*. Since the varied expressions of great poets, with regard to one and the same subject, all attain maturity, the *pāka* consists of the composition of word and sense proper to the development of *rasa*. So it is said: "That is maturity of a sentence [*vākyapāka*] to me by which the mode of stringing together word and sense, according to quality [*guṇa*], rhetorical figure [*alaṃkāra*], mode of diction [*rīti*], and speech in general [*ukti*], is relished [as *rasa*]." And again: "There being the speaker, there being the word, there being the *rasa*, there is not that by which the nectar of words flow." Hence the Yāyāvarīyas [to which school of opinion Rājaśekhara himself appears to have belonged] say: "Since the *pāka*, which is capable of being communicated by word through its inferribility from its effect, is in a high degree the province of denotation [the verbal function of conveying the literal conventional sense], still it is subject to the usage of what is established by the sanction of the critic of sensibility, the *sahṛdaya*."

If this is not verbiage, it may mean that, in Rājaśekhara's opinion, *pāka* is conveyed chiefly through words, and, taken as verbal proficiency, it comes primarily under literalness of sense; but it finds its scope in the sense established by the relisher of *rasa*, the *sahṛdaya*. In other words, we have here the same tendency of relating it ultimately, in accordance with the prevailing theory of *rasa*, to the reproductive appreciation of the reader rather than to the productive imagination of the poet.

It is proper to note in this connexion that the term *pāka*, like the term *rasa*, has a reference to its etymological meaning of physical tasting, with reference to the appreciator, which has been fancifully likened to that resulting from the ripeness of fruits. As such ripeness of fruits bears different kinds of taste, the analysts love to carry the analogy into distinguishing and naming *pākas* after various kinds of fruity taste. Vāmana refers very early to the ripeness of taste corresponding to that borne by the egg-plant (*vṛn-tākapāka*),* but other writers add various designations after a fairly long list of fruits, such as grapes (*drākṣā*), cocoanut (*nārikela*), mango (*sahakāra*), wood-apple (*kapittha*), jujube (*badara*), cucumber (*trapusa*), and even the sour tamarind (*tintiḍi*) and the bitter *Azadirachta indica* (*nimba*).

One may detect in this tendency a lurking hedonistic attitude towards explaining artistic facts. But this is outdone by a similar, but mixed, hedonistic and sexualistic bias of some unsystematic *rasa* theorists like Rudrabhaṭṭa and Bhoja,* who would regard the enjoyment of the erotic sentiment as the sole and proper objective of poetry. Although the *dhvani* theorists* generically classified the different poetic sentiments on the basis of the various natural emotions (like love, laughter, grief, and heroism), they were careful to emphasise the unity of the resulting relish as a simple and indivisible enjoyment, which is not pathological but idealised and serene, and from which every trace of its component or material is obliterated. That is to say, love or grief is not any longer experienced as love or grief, but as pure aesthetic sentiment of bliss evoked by the idealised poetic creation. They are fond of explaining the process under the analogy of a beverage which, made up a black pepper, candied sugar, camphor, and other ingredients, gives us a taste different from its constituents.

The later writers more or less repeat this formula in theory; but some of the unorthodox, eclectic, and less systematic compilers, like Bhoja, did not hesitate to bring out the practical implications of such a realistic description. Love had been the most absorbing and universally appealing theme of Sanskrit poetry and drama, so it is not surprising that they should single out the erotic sentiment, but thereby they erect a mere concomitant into an exclusive essential. To this they naturally add a sexualistic bias supplemented by an elaborate psychology of amatory concepts. This is done with the object, apparently, of guiding the aspiring poet in the composition of erotic pieces so popular and profuse in Sanskrit. The historical condition of the growth of the discipline thus supplied a motive for developing the innate inclination towards artistic hedonism and sexualism, although a theoretic appearance was often given under the all-atoning name of *rasa*.

We have in consequence a prolific series of erotico-rhetorical treatises, beginning with Rudrabhaṭṭa's *Śṛṅgāra-tilaka*,* in which the minute diversities of the amorous condition are elaborately analysed and classified with surprising assiduity and acuteness. Scholastic formalism is manifest here, too, in the making of distinctions and categories, in the analysis of accidents rather than of essentials. But one cannot mistake the obvious implication of this pleasurable eroticism. The attitude was certainly not improved when a religious turn was given by translating this eroticism into a devotional sentiment in the semirhetorical treatises of emotionalist *Vaiṣṇava* devotees, like Rūpa Gosvāmin,* who show a decided leaning towards sensualism of a refined and subtle type.

Despite these aberrations, there is one point on which the complete agreement of the theorists indicates that they undoubtedly had a glimpse of the true character of poetic expression. They refuse to admit that the distinction between prose and poetry lies in an external fact,—metre. They recognise that the distinction is altogether internal.*

According to the nature of the particular intuition, a poet may express himself in prose or in verse. In the one case his intellect predominates, in the other his sentiment; but since the one aspect of the spiritual activity may pass into the other, all prose has a poetical side. The theorists could not apply this idea of the interiority of poetic expression, however, when they admitted the conventional grouping of expressive facts into literary classes (such as romance, story, epic, lyric, or drama) and formulated laws for them. These distinctions are useful; but they are merely abstract or quantitative categories, made for the convenience of logical exposition, by which we analyse, after reflection, the individual expressive facts into a series of relations, moments, or aspects, and which therefore do not affect the nature of the poetic intuition or expression itself. A similar tendency leads the theorists, as we have seen, to analyse and classify the synthetic unity of individual expression into universal rhetorical and other similar categories, a process which reduces an organism into a mechanism. They are thereby prone to collect an imposing array of crude facts and even useful information, but these are often confused, irrelevant, or discordant for the purpose of explaining the nature of poetic creation itself.

It is hardly necessary, therefore, in the discussion of theoretic principle, to linger over the industrious but subtle analysis of a very large crowd of writers who dealt with the rhetorical and other categories as logical facts but, hopelessly mixing them up sometimes with artistic facts, attempted to imply for their study a higher name than rhetoric. No really new or inspiring ideas on the aesthetic question appear in the countless treatises that were composed with immense trouble and subtlety. The husks of pedantry were conscientiously but mistakenly accepted for explaining the juice of poetry. They contain a mass of learned and useful things, an array of pseudo-aesthetic concepts, defined psychically or logically, but which hardly pertain to the fundamental aesthetic problem. Some of the works are gigantic, but they are giants puffed up with commonplaces.

Even those very few writers who felt that some elements of the real problem had been overlooked and wanted to think freely found themselves in the end hopelessly caught in the mazes of conventional beliefs, which landed them in unsurmountable contradictions and perplexities. This is illustrated even by the cases of the two most accomplished systematisers of this group, Mammaṭa* and Viśvanātha.* They attempted to make some variations in the conventional assumptions but merely came out through the gate by which they entered. Even the latest writer of this group, Jagannātha,* who pretended to leave the broad and easy path of mechanical conventionality, accepted in reality most of the established dogmas and formulas. More a polemical reasoner than a constructive contemplator, his erudite distinctions are in most cases trivial niceties. Nevertheless, some of his critiques of previous theories are just and give occasional glimpses of penetration. He remarks with insight that the word alone is important in poetry as giving expression to a charming sense. The charmingness consists in giving an idealised pleasure which is a fact of internal experience. The cause of this pleasure is a conception or a series of representations, consisting of continued contemplation of things characterised by the pleasure itself. This pleasure is specifically different from what one finds in the actually pleasing, and depends upon taste formed by continued contemplation of beautiful objects. The criterion of poetry, therefore, does not lie in its capability of producing the idealised enjoyment of a poetic feeling alone; for the creative imagination may also concern itself with descriptive matter, thought, or ornamentation as its material or stimulus. Although not very clearly formulated, these opinions are remarkable variations of the accepted theory. But the problem of poetic creation is still looked at not from the standpoint of the poet's creating but from that of the reader's recreating; and the mechanical analysis of canons and categories, even if they are related to the reader's idealised enjoyment, persists.

We have now surveyed what, from the viewpoint of aesthetic, is worth while in the speculations of Sanskrit poetics. We cannot but be struck by the smallness of the number of theorists who have seen the nature of the theoretic problem clearly. The majority hardly take poetry as a living discourse, in itself indivisible, among expressive organisms, but consider it as a series of dead abstractions capable of scientific dissection. They demonstrate, in short, a curious confusion of the artistic process with that of natural science. Many incidentally had a flash of the truth and offered just remarks; made conscientious collections and useful analyses of empirical canons. But the main problem is approached from a restricted angle, and has not been formulated clearly or in its entirety.

$$4$$

AESTHETIC ENJOYMENT

THE THEORY OF *rasa*,* like the theory of *dhvani* with which
it is intimately connected, forms one of the most important
aesthetic foundations of Sanskrit poetics. From its first appearance in the dramatic theory of Bharata down to its es-
tablishment as the soul of poetry in the work of Viśvanātha
there has been a steady working out of the idea into a fundamental aesthetic concept.

The *dhvani* school, in its analysis of poetry, found that
the contents of a good poem may generally be distinguished
as either that which is expressed and includes what is given
in so many words or that which is not expressed, but must
be added by the imagination of the reader or the listener.
The unexpressed or suggested part, which is distinctly linked
up with the expressed and which is developed by a peculiar
process of suggestion (*vyañjanā*),* is taken to be the 'soul' or
essence of poetry.

To the grammarians and learned writers, it seemed para-
doxical to state that the very essence of a poem is that
which is not even expressed. On the other hand, some form
of symbolical speech, in which wisdom demands that one
should express oneself more in hints and suggestions than in
actual words, was always in vogue, and the poets had been
more or less partial to the method of speaking in metaphor or wrapping up their ideas in transparent allegories.
But the suggestive poetry is something different from the
merely metaphorical, which Vāmana had already amply
recognised and on which the *alaṃkāra* and the *rīti* schools
had put so much emphasis. The metaphorical or the alle-
goric, however veiled it may be, is still in a sense expressed
and must be taken as such. The suggested sense (*vyaṅgya*)
is always unexpressed and is therefore a source of greater

charm through its capacity of concealment; for this concealment, in which lies the essence of art, is in reality no
concealment at all. The new aesthetic school claims a particular function of suggestion, appertaining to words and
their senses, whereby the unexpressed or the inexpressible
is called into being, or, to speak with Kant, whereby poetry
becomes an expression of 'the aesthetic idea'.

Now the unexpressed, through the suggestive power of
word or idea, may be an unexpressed thought or matter
(*vastu*) or an unexpressed figure of speech (*alaṃkāra*),
but in most cases it is a mood or feeling (*rasa*) which is
inexpressible directly.* The *dhvani* school took up the moods
and feelings as an element of the unexpressed and tried to
harmonise the idea of *rasa* with the theory of *dhvani*. It was
realised that poetry was not, as Daṇḍin thought, the mere
clothing of agreeable ideas in agreeable language; feelings
and moods play an important part in it. But feelings and
moods in themselves are inexpressible. We can give a name
to them, but naming a mood or feeling is not equivalent to
expressing or developing it. At best, therefore, we can suggest it. What the poet can directly express or describe are
the *vibhāvas*, etc.;* but with the help of these expressed elements, which must be generalised and conceived not as they
appear in the mundane world but as they may be imagined
in a poetic world, the poet can awaken in us, through the
power of suggestion inherent in words or ideas, a particular
alaukika condition of the soul in which the relish of the
feeling is possible. To be sure, the poet cannot rouse the
same mood or feeling as the person (*e.g.*, Rāma) whom he
describes felt in times past, but he can call up a reflection
of it which is similar in some respects; and this condition
of enjoyment in the reader's soul is the relish of *rasa*, which
can be brought into consciousness by the power of suggestion inherent in words and their sense.

Here arises the new aspect given to the *rasa* theory by
the exponents of the *dhvani* school. They interpret Bharata's
much-discussed dictum to mean that *rasa* is suggested by
the union of the permanent mood with the *vibhāvas* through
the relation of the suggested (*vyaṅgya*) and the suggestor

(*vyañjaka*); and that the *niṣpatti* of Bharata's *sūtra* should mean *abhivyakti.* Commenting on Bhaṭṭa Nāyaka's theory, Abhinavagupta points out that there is no need, as there is no authority, for assuming the two powers of *bhāvakatva* and *bhogīkarana;* for they are implicitly included in the idea of *rasavyañjanā* and its ultimate *āsvāda.* Bharata's dictum *kāvyārthān bhāvayantīti bhāvāḥ* implies *bhāvakatva* to be an inherent capacity of all *bhāvas* as the cause of existence (*bhū iti karaṇe dhātuḥ*) or the diffusion (*vyāptyartham*) of the sense of poetry, the sense indicating the principal sense consisting of the relish of *rasa*. Hence the *sthāyin,* together with the *vyabhicārin*, being *bhāvas* themselves, bring into existence through this inherent power the extraordinary relishable sense of poetry, cognised in a general form (*sarvasādhāraṇatayā āsvādayati*). In this way the *sthāyin*, or even the *kāvya* itself, may be regarded generally as the *bhāvaka* or *niṣpādaka* of *rasa;* and this so-called *bhāvakatva*, according to Abhinava consists in nothing more than a suitable use of *guṇa* and *alaṃkāra* for the ultimate purpose of awakening *rasa* through the suggestive power of word and sense.

Thus disposing of the power of *bhāvakatva*, Abhinava turns to the other power assumed as *bhoga* or *bhogīkaraṇa* by Bhaṭṭa Nāyaka. He remarks that beyond the *pratīti* or perception of *rasa*, he is not aware of any other process called *bhoga*. If it is relish or enjoyment, it is already admitted; and nothing is gained by giving it a new name, just as nothing is gained by arriving at the same idea by the use of different terms like *darśana, anumiti, śruti, upamiti*, or *pratibhāna*, according only to the distinction of the means employed. Hence *bhoga* is nothing more than the perception of *rasa*, consisting of its essence of relish, based on permanent moods like *rati*, etc. But it must not be supposed to rest there; for although it is admitted that wherever there is *rasa* there is no doubt its perception, consisting in its enjoyment, yet since the nature of *sattva* and other *guṇas* involved in such enjoyment is diversified, according as they are principal or subordinate, and is therefore in itself infinite and incomprehensible, the relish of *rasa* is not to be measured by the mere supposition of three functions. The *bhoga*, supposed by Bhaṭṭa Nāyaka, consists, therefore, essentially in the *āsvāda* of *rasa*, possible because of the suggestive power of poetry; and, falling naturally within poetry's domain, it need not be taken as a separate function.

This, in general outline, is the theory of *dhvani* and *rasa* finally reached by Sanskrit poetics. The chief value of its contribution lies in its recognition, foreshadowed by Bhaṭṭa Nāyaka, of the poetic sentiment as a fact of internal aesthetic experience and of its process of idealisation from a natural feeling (*bhāva*) to a poetic emotion (*rasa*). In this the theorists undoubtedly approach the very core of the aesthetic problem, and solve the question of *śabdārthasāhitya* in a novel way.

Unfortunately, the starting limitations persist, preventing the development of mere rhetoric into aesthetic. Because of these limitations it cannot be maintained that these theorists have said the last word on the subject, or said it clearly and consistently; but they have certainly dealt with some of its fundamental aspects very ably. A suitable exposition is given indeed of the aesthetic enjoyment resulting from the idealised creation of poetry, and incidentally of the general nature of poetic idealisation, but the question is still approached from the standpoint of the reader or critic, the *sāmājika* or *sahṛdaya*.* The problem of poetic intuition from the point of view of the poet's mind is not considered in its entirety. The process is reversed; the theory speaks of reader's reproduction, and not of poet's production. It speaks of the *sāmājika's* relation to the poetic creation, and goes on to determine its character as an aesthetic fact solely from the point of view of its aesthetic enjoyment by the *sāmājika*. But it does not speak of the relation of the poet's mind to his creation by starting from the consideration of the creative imagination and its automatic externalisation as an aesthetic fact.

The theory of *rasa* is thus essentially one of aesthetic enjoyment. The *pratīti* of *rasa*, Abhinava maintains, is nothing more than its manifestation (*abhivyakti*) by the power of suggestion, resulting in an extraordinary state of relish, known as *rasanā, āsvāda,* or *carvanā.* What is manifested is not the *rasa* itself, but its relish; not the mood itself, but its reflection in the form of a subjective condition of aesthetic enjoyment in the reader. This taste or relish partakes, no doubt, of the nature of cognition; it is nevertheless different from the ordinary (*laukika**) forms of the process, because its means, the *vibhāvas,* are not to be taken as ordinary causes.

This will make it clear why *rasas* like *karuṇa, bībhatsa,* or *bhayānaka,* which cause pity, disgust, or horror, should be termed *rasa,* in which enjoyment is essential.* The relish of *rasa* is supposed to be an extraordinary bliss, not to be likened to ordinary pain or pleasure, and the mind is so entirely lost in it that even when the sentiment of grief or horror is relished in such a state, pain is never felt, and even when it is felt it is a pleasurable pain. The fact is borne out by the common experience that when grief is represented, the spectator or the reader says, "I have enjoyed it." Hence Viśvanātha* remarks that when consigned to poetry and dramatic representation those very things which are called causes of pain in the world (like banishment of Sītā in the forest) possess the right to be called, in consequence of their assuming such a function, *alaukikavibhāvas,* etc., and from them only pleasure ensues, as it does from bites and the like in amorous dalliance. It is also maintained that tears constitute no proof that anything but pleasure is felt in poetry; for the tears which are shed by the reader are not those of pain but those of sentiment. Jagannātha's* remarks in this connexion are interesting. He says that the shedding of tears and the like are due to the nature of the experience of the particular pleasure, and not to pain. When tears arise in a devotee on listening to a description of the deity, there is not the slightest feeling of pain. Such is the power of the extraordinary function of poetry that even unpleasant things like sorrow generate *alaukika* pleasure, and this pleasant aesthetic relish should be distinguished from the experience realised by other, ordinary means.

Although *rasa* requires these factors for its manifestation and cannot exist without them, it cannot yet be regarded as an ordinary effect, and the cause-and-effect theory is inapplicable. For in the transcendental sphere of poetry, the connexion between cause and effect gives place to an imaginative system of relations, which has the power of stirring the reader's soul into *rasa*. The resulting *rasa* cannot be identified with its constituent *vibhāvas*,* for the latter are not experienced separately, but the whole appears as *rasa*, which is thus simple and indivisible; and at the time of relish nothing else but *rasa* is raised to our consciousness. The writers on poetics are fond of explaining this phenomenon under the analogy, mentioned earlier, of a beverage, made up of black pepper, candied sugar, camphor, and other ingredients, which gives us a different taste from that of its constituents. The result, therefore, is an indissoluble unity of taste from which every trace of the constituent elements is obliterated.

Abhinavagupta goes a step further in maintaining that the *sthāyin* (permanent mood) inferred from its *laukika* causes (*e.g.*, woman, garden, etc.) remains in the hearts of the appreciating audience in the subtle form of latent impressions. On reading a poem or witnessing a drama this permanent mood, remaining in the form of latent impressions (*vāsanā*), is suggested by the depicted *vibhāvas*, etc., which cease to be called *laukika* causes but go by the name of *vibhāvas*, etc., in poetry and drama, and which are taken in their general form without specific connexions. The *vibhāvas* are generalized in the minds of the reader and do not refer to particularities, not through the power of *bhāvakatva*, as supposed by Bhaṭṭa Nāyaka, but generally through the suggestive power of word and sense and specifically through a skilful use of *guṇa* and *alaṃkāra* in poetry and clever representation in the drama. In the same way, the *sthāyibhāva* (permanent mood), which is the source of the *rasa*, is also generalised, because the germ of it is already existent in the reader's soul in the form of impressions; and this generalisation, together with the beauty of the generalised representation of the *vibhāvas*, etc., removes all temporal and spatial limitations. The mood is generalised also in the sense that it refers not to any particular reader but to readers in general, so that, although it is relished by a particular individual, at the time of relishing it he does not think that it is relished by him alone, but by all persons of poetic sensibility. This relish is known as *rasa* in poetry and drama.

The effectiveness of poetry depends, then, upon latent impressions of feelings which we once went through. These are roused when we read a poem which describes similar things by universal sympathy (*sādhāraṇya* or *sādhāraṇī-karaṇa*).* Those who have never experienced the feeling of love, for instance, and have therefore no impression of experience left in them, as well as those who have no sense of community of human feelings can never relish *rasa* in poetry. The *vāsanā*, we are told, is natural (*svābhāvikī* or *nai-sargikī*),* but it may be acquired by study and experience. The writers on poetics are merciless in their satire on dull grammarians and old *mīmāṃsakas*, to whom such relish of *rasa* is denied, and they declare unanimously that *rasikā eva rasāsvāde yogyāḥ*.* As *rasa* is not an objective entity which can reside in the hero or the actor, it is realised, as Dhanañjaya* puts it, by the reader's own capacity of enjoyment. Thus a degree of culture and aesthetic instinct is demanded in the critic, the *rasika* or *sahṛdaya*, who is the *adhikārin*,* dignified with the appellation of *pramātṛ*,* compatible with this subtle and extraordinary conception of poetry. As Abhinavagupta puts it: *adhikārī cātra vimala-pratibhānaśālihṛdayaḥ;*° and elsewhere he describes such a *sahṛdaya* as *yeṣāṃ kāvyānuśīlanābhyāsavaśād viśadībhūte manomukure varṇanīyatanmayībhavanayogyatā te hṛdaya-saṃvādabhājaḥ sahṛdayāḥ*.*

This subtle conception of *rasa* makes it difficult to express the notion properly in Western critical terminology. The word has been translated etymologically by the terms flavour, relish, gustation, taste, *Geschmack*, or *saveur*; but none of these renderings seems to be adequate. 'Mood', or the term '*Stimmung*' used by Jacobi, may be the nearest approach to it, but the concept has hardly any analogy in European critical theories. Most of the terms employed have ideational associations of their own, and are therefore not strictly applicable. For instance, 'taste' and 'relish', though literally correct, must not be understood to imply aesthetic or moral judgement, 'good' or 'bad' taste, but must be taken to indicate an idea similar to what we mean when we speak of tasting food. At the same time, this realistic description must not lead us to drag it down to the level of a bodily pleasure; for this artistic pleasure is given as almost equivalent to the philosophic bliss, known as *ānanda*, being lifted above worldly joy.

This peculiar condition of the ego, the *rasa*, is realised through the characteristic function of *vyañjanā* (suggestion) in poetry. The idea is elaborated by later theorists, who take pains to show that it does not come under the province of *abhidhā* (denotation), nor of *tātparya* (import), nor of *lakṣaṇā* (indication), nor of *pratyakṣa* (perception), nor of *anumāna* (inference), nor of *smaraṇa* (reminiscence), admitted by philosophers and grammarians. Into these technicalities, which properly come under the discussion of the *vyañjanāvṛtti*,* we need not enter. But it may be noted that Abhinava describes this *abhivyakti*, which is taken as synonymous with *carvaṇā*, as *vītavighnapratīti*, cognition rendered free from obstacles. Following him, Jagannātha notes in this connexion: *vyaktiś ca bhagnāvaraṇā cit, yathā hi śarāvādinā pihito dīpas tannivṛttau saṃnihitān padārthān prakāśayati, svayaṃ ca prakāśate, evam ātmacaitanyaṃ vibhāvādisaṃvalitān ratyādīn.* Similarly, *carvaṇā* is described by the author of the *Prabhā** as *vibhāvādisamūhālambanena ratyavacchinnā caitanyābhivyaktiś carvaṇā, sā ca bhagnāvaraṇā cit.** The cognition of *rasa*, therefore, is a distinct realisation freed from all doubts and obstacles by means of the *vibhāvas*, etc., which are accordingly designated as *vighnāpasāraka*.* It is variously described as *camatkāranirveśa* (awakening of poetic charm), *rasanā* (relish), *āsvāda* (taste), *bhoga* (fruition), *samāpatti* (accomplishment), *laya* (fusion), and *viśrānti* (repose).

The essence of *rasa*, therefore, consists in its *āsvāda* or *carvaṇā* (*carvyamāṇaikaprāṇaḥ*) which is *alaukika*, being incompassable by the ordinary processes of knowledge. It is

a relish in which the *rasa* alone, apart from its constituent
elements, is raised to consciousness; and it is, therefore, described as a relish in which the contemplation of any other
thing but *rasa* itself is lost (*vigalitavedyāntara*) or which
is free from the contact of aught else perceived (*vedyāntarasparśaśūnya*), like the state of mind lost in the philosophic
contemplation of Brahma. It is not capable of proof or designation and cannot be made known, for its perception is inseparable from its existence, it is identical with the knowledge itself.

The only proof of the existence of *rasa* is its relish itself
by the *sahṛdaya*. It is, therefore, *sakalasahṛdayasaṃvā-
dabhājā pramātrā gocarīkṛtaḥ.*° Although it is a very intimate relish, *camatkāra* is supposed to constitute its life
breath. This *camatkāra*, which has been compared to the
'wonder-spirit' of modern critics, is described by Viśvanātha
as a kind of expanding of the mind, of which another name
is 'wonder' (*camatkāraś cittavistārarūpo vismayāpara-
paryāyaḥ*°), implying that the marvellous always underlies
the *rasa* (*tac camatkārasāratve sarvatrāpy adbhuto rasaḥ*°).
Jagannātha, however, completes the idea by correlating this
camatkāra with the *vaicitrya* or *vicchitti* of the *alaṃkāra*
school, who mean by it a special charm, due to an act of
imagination on the part of the poet (*kavikarma* or *kavipratibhā*°) underlying and constituting the essence of all poetic figures. The *camatkāra*, therefore, which is the essence
of all poetic figures, is also the essence of *rasa*, and has been
defined as a fact of our consciousness (*anubhavasākṣika*),
consisting of extraordinary pleasure (*alaukikāhlāda*) which
depends on a concept formed by continued contemplation
of itself.

The last step in this idea was taken by the attempt to
bring poetry to the level of religion by likening aesthetic
enjoyment to the ecstatic bliss of divine contemplation
(*brahmāsvāda*). Viśvanātha sums up the idea briefly thus:
The *rasa*, arising from the exaltation of *sattva* (purity),
indivisible, self-manifested, made up of joy and thought in
their identity, free from the contact of aught else perceived,
akin to the realisation of Brahma, the life whereof is super-

mundane wonder, is enjoyed by those competent in in-
separableness (of the object from the realisation thereof)
and, as it were, in its own shape. It follows from this that
the *pramātṛ*, to whom alone this bliss is vouchsafed, is like
a *yogin* (devotee) who deserves this preference through his
accumulated merits (*puṇyavantaḥ pramiṇvanti yogivad
rasasaṃtatim**).

This, in its general outlines, is the rasa theory as finally
fixed by the *dhvani* school. All later writers, from Dhanañjaya to Jagannātha, accept this new interpretation and
attempt to work it out in detail. Thus, an endeavour was
made not only to explain the concept of *rasa* in terms of
inward experience, but also to absorb this idea of aesthetic
delectation into the new theory of *dhvani* and make it applicable to poetry.

The *rasa* school began to merge from this time onwards
into the dominant *dhvani* school. Even Mahimabhaṭṭa,* who
attempted to demolish the *dhvani* theory, was forced to ac-
knowledge *rasa* and declare that there was no difference of
opinion between himself and the *Dhvanikāra* on this point,
that they differed only with regard to the function *par
excellence* which should be operative in poetry. But the
dhvani school* and its followers consider *rasa* as an element of the unexpressed only: and, although their theory in
putting a great emphasis on *rasadhvani* all but leads to such
a conclusion, both the *Dhvanikāra* and Ānandavardhana are
yet careful not to erect it into the very 'soul' of poetry. From
the theoretical standpoint at least, they could not give exclusive preference to *rasadhvani*, however important it may
be. For, in their complete scheme of poetics, the unexpressed may also take the form of *vastudhvani* and
alaṃkāradhvani,* and the centre of gravity in a poem may
lie in its matter or in its poetic figure as well as in its *rasa*.

Abhinavagupta, however, appears to have attached little
weight to these theoretical considerations. Brushing them
aside, he boldly brings forward the essentiality of *rasa*, de-
claring that there can be no poetry without it (*na hi ta-
cchūnyaṃ kāvyaṃ kiṃcid asti*) because all poetry lives

through *rasa* (*rasenaiva sarvaṃ jīvati kāvyam*). He attempts, however, to reconcile the theoretical discrepancy by saying that although the unexpressed may also take the form of a *vastu* or an *alaṃkāra*, these two kinds of suggestion resolve themselves ultimately into the suggestion of *rasa*, which is in fact the essence of poetry.

This view apparently led Viśvanātha to push the theory to its logical limit and formulate his somewhat extreme proposition that the *rasa* alone constitutes the essence of poetry. But the considerations which led the founders of the *dhvani* theory to leave this view wisely unstated could not be easily put out of the way. Jagannātha objects on this very ground. The definition of poetry given by Viśvanātha, he says, cannot be accepted. It would exclude as poetry that in which the central charm lies in the matter or in the poetic figure (*e.g.*, in professedly descriptive and ornamental poetry), and such an exclusion is warranted neither by theory nor by the practice of great poets. Viśvanātha had anticipated this objection, saying that in these cases there is a semblance of *rasa* (*rasābhāsa*), and the verse given in *Dhvanyāloka* as an instance of *vastudhvani* is, in his opinion, admissible because there is a touch of *rasa* (*rasa-sparśa*) and not because mere *vyaṅgyavastu* can constitute the essence of poetry. But Jagannātha argues that nothing is gained by this clumsy subterfuge of an indirect reference to *rasa*. Such a reference may also be construed in phrases like 'the cow moves' or 'the deer leaps'. This omnipresent *rasa* cannot be taken as a criterion; to do so would reduce any and every content of poetry to the position of a *vibhāva*, *anubhāva*, or *vyabhicāribhāva* of the *rasa*.

Jagannātha himself, one of the latest writers on the subject, tries to solve the difficulty by studiously avoiding all mention of *rasa* in his definition of poetry, although in theory he, like Viśvanātha, adheres in the main to the views of the *dhvani* school. Jagannātha mentions as many as eight different theories about *rasa*, but the existence of so many conflicting views, as well as the fact that *rasa* cannot be taken as the essence of all poetry, leads him to define poetry as *ramaṇīyārthapratipādakaḥ śabdaḥ*,* inasmuch as all theorists agree that *rasa*, which cannot be manifested without an accompanying state of joy, conveys a peculiar *ramaṇīyatā* essential to poetry.* It will be noticed, therefore, that recognition was refused to any attempt, like that of Viśvanātha, to develop the theory further out of itself; and the views of the *dhvani* school, as represented later by Mammaṭa,* became, in spite of many attempts at improvement in detail, a kind of canonical code for all future time.

In spite of the unquestioned dominance of the *dhvani* school, which amply recognised *rasa* but regarded it as one of the phases of the unexpressed in poetry, one class of writers* still adhered to *rasa* as the only element worth considering in poetry, although they never theoretically discussed the position and, like Viśvanātha, built up a system on its basis. Of all the *rasas*, however, as *śṛṅgāra* (love) forms the absorbing theme of Sanskrit poetry and drama in general, and as this particular poetic mood possesses an almost universal appeal, these writers naturally work out the *śṛṅgāra* in all its detail.

We have, in consequence, a body of erotico-rhetorical treatises, of which the earliest and the most remarkable is Rudrabhaṭṭa's *Śṛṅgāratilaka*,* one of whose avowed objects is to apply the idea of *rasa*, already discussed in connexion with the drama by Bharata and others, to poetry. Following this we have Bhoja's *Śṛṅgāraprakāśa*,* cited by Vidyādhara* and Kumārasvāmin,* which deals with the subject in the usual elaborate cyclopaedic manner of its author, with profuse illustrations of every phase of the sentiment, in no less than twenty chapters. After this come innumerable works of a similar nature, which take *rasa*, especially *śṛṅgāra*, as their principal theme, and which were composed with the apparent object of guiding the poet in the composition of the erotic pieces so popular and profuse in Sanskrit poetry. Of these, the *Bhāvaprakāśa* of Śāradātanaya, which reproduces the substance of most of the chapters of Bhoja's work, the *Rasārṇava* of Siṅgabhūpāla, and the two well-known works of Bhānudatta, the *Rasamañjarī* and *Rasataraṅgiṇī*, deserve mention. None of these specialised treatises, however, add anything of speculative interest to a topic already thrashed out to its extreme; and as they belong properly to the province of Erotics rather than Poetics, a treatment of them must be sought elsewhere. The simple idea elaborated more or less in all these works is that the fundamental *rasa* is *śṛṅgāra*, which is consequently treated in detail with regard to its *vibhāvas*, etc. This brings in the extensive discussion of *nāyaka* and *nāyikā** and their various conditions and emotions acting as a factor of the *rasa*. These works repeat elaborate definitions, distinctions, and classifications of the amatory sentiment with its varying emotional moods and situations, matters which seem frequently to exercise great attraction for the mediaeval scholastic mind. These theorists delight in arranging into divisions and sub-divisions, according to rank, character, circumstances, and the like, all conceivable types of the hero, the heroine, and their adjuncts, together with the different shades of gestures, graces, feelings, moods, and emotions, in conformity to the tradition which had already obtained in the sphere of dramaturgy. We cannot deny that these essays indicate subtle power of analysis and insight, and, although much of it is marked by scholastic formalism, there is an un-mistakable attempt to do justice to facts, not only as they appear to experience but to the observation of general poetic usage. In the elaborate working out of the general thesis that the *rasa* is evolved on the basis of one or another of what they call the 'permanent mental moods' with the help of various emotional adjuncts, these writers proceeded a long way in the careful analysis of poetic emotions, the psychology of which bears an intimate relation to their theory and in itself deserves separate study.

A new turn was given to the theory fy Rūpa Gosvāmin's *Ujjvalanīlamaṇi,** which brings erotico-religious ideas to bear upon the general theme of *rasa*. It attempts to deal with *rasa* in terms of the Vaiṣṇava idea of *ujjvala** or *madhura-rasa,** by which is meant the *śṛṅgārarasa*, the term *ujjvala* being apparently suggested by Bharata's description of the rasa.* The *madhurarasa*, however, is represented not in its secular aspect but primarily as a phase of *bhaktirasa* (*mad-*

hurākhyo bhaktirasaḥ);* for the *Vaiṣṇava* theology admits five *rasas* as forming roughly the five degrees or aspects of the realisation of *bhakti* (faith): *śānta* (tranquility), *dāsya* (also called *prīti*, servitude or humility), *sakhya* (also called *preyas*, friendship or equality), *vātsalya* (parental affection), and *mādhurya* (sweetness).* The last, also called the *ujjvalarasa*, being the principal, is termed *bhaktirasarāṭ** and constitutes, as such, the subjectmatter of the present treatise. The *Kṛṣṇarati* (love of Kṛṣṇa) forms the *sthāyibhāva** of this *rasa*, and the recipient here is not the literary *sahṛdaya* but the *bhakta*, the faithful. This *sthāyibhāva*, known as *madhurarati*, which is the source of this particular rasa, is defined in terms of love of Kṛṣṇa; and the nature of the *nāyaka* and *nāyikā* is defined in the same manner, and their feelings and emotions illustrated by examples adduced from poems dealing with the love stories of Kṛṣṇa and Rādhā. The work is, therefore, essentially a *Vaiṣṇava* religious treatise, presented in a literary garb, taking Kṛṣṇa as the ideal hero, with the caution, however, that what is true of Kṛṣṇa as the hero does not apply to the ordinary secular hero.

5

CREATION AND RE-CREATION

ONE OF THE great Sanskrit poets, distressed probably by the capricious antipathy of contemporary critical judgement, declared that there was or would arise some kindred spirit who would do justice to his work, for time was boundless and the world was wide. Since then, many a disappointed poet must have wished that time were more boundless and the world were wider. To a poet, his poetic activity is not a caprice or a pastime, but a spiritual necessity. Nothing is more unfortunate for him than being placed among of uncongenial spirits.

In this apparently proud assertion, Bhavabhūti has unerringly declared that the only true criterion of aesthetic judgement, as of all other kinds of judgement, is this: that an activity which is spiritual can be recognised only by an identical spiritual activity. What the poet expresses is a state of his soul; it can produce no effect except on souls kindred to it, prepared to receive it. In order to judge a work of art, the true critic must place himself in the poet's position or point of view. If the poet creates, the critic must re-create; and the judicial activity, being reproductive, is essentially identical with the productive; the only difference lies in the diversity of circumstances, in the one being assertive and the other receptive.

To deny this substantial identity of spirit denies the possibility of the poet to communicate or the critic to judge. Self-expression would be meaningless if it does not find an echo in other selves. Unless we place ourselves ideally in the same condition, how can we receive and judge what is outside ourselves? In popular parlance, the creative intuition is called genius, the recreative, taste; the difference between the two aspects of the same spiritual activity cannot be qualitative but is only quantitative and circumstantial. A superman is also a man; genius is not something above or beyond humanity. When we say that the poet sees more clearly than we do, we imply that he has a more complete intuition of things. The ordinary intuition does not differ in its nature from the poetic; but poets possess in a larger degree an aptitude for expressing fully certain complex states of the soul. In this identity lies the possibility of true aesthetic appreciation and estimate, the possibility of our little souls uniting in spirit with great souls and becoming great with them.

The man of taste is known in Sanskrit theory as the *sahṛdaya*,* who is regarded as the final court of appeal in all artistic matters. Abhinavagupta lays down clearly that, apart from culture and technical knowledge, the *sahṛdaya* must possess the capacity of identifying himself with the poetic creation (*varṇanīyatanmayībhavanayogyatā*). It must be understood that empirically the critic and the poet are not the same, but by the process of idealised contemplation his spirit can be one with that of the poet. That the process is not one of mere understanding is made clear by the observation that the *sahṛdaya* is not a mere intellectual cogniser (*boddhṛ*), but an enjoyer of the idealised bliss produced in his soul by the poetic creation (*rasayitṛ*).* Abhinavagupta also recognises that there may be disturbing elements due to prejudice, perversion, and ignorance; but in the true critic these are eliminated by knowledge and culture, and the mirror of his mind becomes free and clear (*viśadībhūtamanomukura**). If a critic could always achieve this state, he would, as a kindred spirit, appreciate the poet's work as it really is, and it would not then be necessary to leave it to posterity to award the palm as a more dispassionate judge.

The conditions of production and reproduction are not always identical, however. Neither the stimulants nor the psychic dispositions remain constant, but are always conditioned by time and place. Even the poet himself may not in his old age possess the same psychological condition of physical stimulus for appreciating what he had himself produced in his youth. Hence there is always scope for honest diversities of judgement. Nevertheless, the conditions being ideally equal, there is no justification for the common view that criticism is capricious, depending on personal likes and dislikes. Apart from the question of apathy or animosity, the consideration of what pleases or displeases is only practical and utilitarian, and has no application to purely aesthetic judgement. Those who maintain that literary taste is only relative are often led by the etymology of the word * to the perplexing mistake of tracing it to a merely gustatory origin. The Sanskrit theorists speak of relish (*rasanā*), taste (*āsvāda*), and gustation (*carvaṇā*), but they seldom fall into error of regarding the appreciation of the *sahṛdaya* as a practical activity of personal pleasure or pain; they take it as a mental condition of idealised bliss evoked by the idealised creation of the poet.

Since to judge is to reproduce, under identical conditions, what the poet produces, it follows that the vision of the poet and that of the critic can never, theoretically, diverge. If the poet sees clearly, the critic must do the same, and regard the work as perfect; if the poet does not see clearly, the critic necessarily does the same and pronounces the work to be imperfect. If the poet sometimes disagrees with the latter judgement, it is only because he does not always realise how he has seen and what he has produced. The difference is honest, but entirely erroneous. Examples are not rare for poets, after the spontaneity of production, in later moments of conscious reflection, to think little of what they produced successfully; and in their attempt to undo what they have done well, they sometimes do worse. This is often due to the disturbing elements spoken of above, but more often to failure to reproduce a previous intuition. The common observation that poets are often bad judges of their own work is not wholly untrue.

If the creative act is really creative, it will be always recognised as such. Like all other forms of spiritual activity, such as the intellectual or the moral, the intuitive activity is in this sense absolute. It is possible, therefore, to affirm an absolute standard of critical taste, which identifies itself absolutely with the poetic genius. But the standard is not absolute in the sense that we can lay down absolute rules and models, elaborated by reasoning into abstract universals, for each creative fact is an individual occurrence which must be judged by itself.

Sanskrit poetics, then, accepts the fundamental position that true criticism implies idealised reconstruction in the reader's soul of what is expressed of the poet's soul. All its notable theories revolve around and appeal ultimately to the appreciation of the man of poetic sensibility, the *sahṛdaya*. The justification of true poetry, in their opinion, lies in its being thus recognised. Even if the different theorists approach the problem through different avenues of thought, they agree in having their assumptions of *guṇa-rīti, vakrokti, pāka, dhvani*, and *rasa* vouched for by the taste of the *sahṛdaya*. By this they clearly indicate the spiritual character of the poetic activity which must be justified by a similar spiritual activity. When they distinguish from physical or logical relations the aesthetic facts which dissolve into an imaginative system of relations, they want to imply that an imaginative fact must be solved and established by an imaginative fact, and not by reason or other extraneous practical considerations.

The Sanskrit theorists thus evince a marvellous aesthetic acumen by emphasising the purely spiritual character of poetic activity, which in its essence is autonomous, independent of intellectuality, utility, or morality. They never regard poetry, on the one hand, as an amusement, superfluity, or frivolity, nor, on the other, as a medium of mere thought or moral maxims. They assume it to be an activity which belongs to the intuitive sphere of the unfettered spirit. Although they do not discuss the question, they at the same time tacitly distinguish the poetic activity from the intellectual or the practical. They evince a strong commonsense by never confusing a poetic with a scientific or didactic work, the *kāvya* with the *śāstra* or the *nīti*. It is curious that these theorists expend a great deal of dogmatic, abstract, and intellectualistic erudition on a cold and monotonously inflated rhetoric—and yet they enjoy poetry as poetry and hardly ever think of the moral end or the intellectual gain.

It became conventional, as it were, for theorists to give long lists of extraneous 'objects' of poetry, but since these so-called objects never intrude upon or seriously affect the shaping of the poetic theories, the enumerations are of little theoretic value. We are told that the chief objects of poetry, from the standpoint of the poet, are wealth, fame, social success, escape from ills; on the reader's side we have delight, solace, instruction in knowledge, proficiency in the arts and ways of the world, and incentive to virtuous conduct. These are sometimes summarily comprehended by the term *trivarga*, that is, the threefold ideal of profit, pleasure, and virtue. To these is sometimes added salvation, completing the *caturvarga*, the fourfold *summum bonum* of life.

This is probably a kind of snobbish attempt to bring poetry on a level with the arts or sciences which solemnly profess such ends. Or the effort may indicate that all poetry at one time was popularly esteemed for its didactic purpose. Thus, we have, on the one hand, an enumeration of the teaching and ennobling functions of poetry; on the other, an insistence on its function of pleasing. There was also a tendency to combine the two duties of teaching and pleasing by supposing that poetry, as distinguished from science and scripture, is like the teaching of a beloved mistress. A poetic composition is regarded as a kind of pleasing fiction containing many useful truths. Aśvaghoṣa speaks similarly of the honey of poetry which makes the bitter drug of doctrine palatable.* Thus poetry appears in turn or in combination as pedagogue, moralist, and seductive mistress. While all these predilections were always there, they fortunately very seldom moulded the theories themselves, which regarded, as they should, the poetic activity apart from such extraneous activities.

In Sanskrit, then, intellectualist poetics, valuing poetry for the knowledge it brought and regarding it as a kind of semi-*śāstra* or semiscience, hardly developed. Nor was there, in spite of sporadic hedonistic tendencies, a practicist poetics emphasising such practical forms of human activity as have a utilitarian, hedonistic, or moralistic end in view. It is clearly indicated, on the other hand, that poetry is not a mere medium of a mass of popularised truths, nor a manifestation of empirical pleasure and pain from the ethical or practical point of view, but that it conveys a state of the soul in its intuitive purity, which can be reproduced in an idealised form in the reader's soul.

Governed entirely by pure imagination, poetry is not the sum of knowledge, sensation, or feeling, but its image, its dream, its intuition, not in a universal but in an individualised shape. What intellect apprehends in abstraction, intuition experiences in immediate concreteness. An apprehension of a fine landscape or a charming smile is a particular state of the soul, for there is nothing beautiful 'outside' in the abstract but what the human spirit makes concretely beautiful. As there is no dualism in the spirit, intellect and intuition are indeed indissolubly linked; but an impression or an intellective fact dissolved in the intuitive, no longer remains as such but becomes an element of intuition. In experiencing the image of a picture or a poem, no one takes it as a series of impressions, some mediate and some immediate; the whole is taken in synthetically, without such distinction. A work of art may contain various elements of knowledge or concepts, but as an organic whole it is purely and entirely an intuitive fact. If its parts are mechanically analysed, it is possible to separate the concepts. But this process destroys the individual unity of the spirit and sublates it into an abstract universal.

The poetic expression as such is indivisible. It does not predicate universal logical truth or falsehood, but individual images, desires, and aspirations unified by intuition in its directness and purity of apprehension. It is in the result produced, method followed, or effect desired that a work of science differs from a work of art; but the one may pass into the other as we may pass from the intellective to the intuitive, and *vice versa*. The intuitive apprehension or formation, which gives us a work of art, stands by itself. It

is as independent of conceptual or pedagogic knowledge
as of various extraneous practical considerations, narcotic,
moralistic, or utilitarian. We are all selective of our intui-
tions in the sense that we do not externalise all of them;
but when we allow our selection to be guided by the educa-
tional, practical, or moral conditions of life, we impose or
attach them to pure aesthetic facts, and a different extraneous end or value is brought in.

The question of truth or untruth, sincerity or insincerity,
virtue or viciousness can arise in only poetry when these
ulterior intellectualist or practicist tendencies intrude. The
only meaning of 'sincerity' admissible in art as art is the
clarity and fulness of intuition and expression. The moral
value of a poetical work has nothing to do with its artistic
value, but is a value in itself and can be justified as such.
But it should not be imposed on art as art. The Sanskrit
theorists appear to recognise this, when, for instance, they
approach the question of indecency (*aślīla*) mainly as
marring the pleasing effect of expression, and not from
that of its ethical significance. This does not mean they
depreciate moral values or make a concession to immorality.
If lies or perversions are in the poet's mind, he will probably
give expression to them; but that is a matter for the moral
judge or the police, and not for the aesthetic critic. If they
are artistic facts, they cannot be lies or perversions for that
very reason. If, on the other hand, the work is not an artistic fact but simply propaganda for evil or immoral ends,
then let moral judgement be invoked by all means, and
proper disciplinary measures be taken.

These questions are indeed not explicitly discussed by the
Sanskrit theorists, but their whole attitude towards poetry
shows that they implicitly accepted them. We have noted
that they display a positivist attitude in elaborating an
empirical aesthetic; but, curiously enough, in spite of conventional protestations of specific extraneous objects of
poetry, they never refuse to believe in the ideal character
of the poetic activity and its purity and freedom from educa-
tive, ethical, or other forms of the practical activity of the
spirit. They appear to recognise that an impression experi-

enced or a feeling felt cannot be experienced or felt again, because nothing in this world happens more than once, but that it is possible for poetry to reproduce the momentary individual situation ideally. The created image in the synthesis of the spirit is ideal and yet real; it is lost in time and space, yet can be produced and contemplated, again and again, from every point of time and space. They say, therefore, that it does not belong to the world (*laukika*) but to the superworld (*alaukika*). The famous opening verse of the *Kāvyaprakāśa* makes this clear when it describes poetic speech as comprehending a creation ungoverned by nature's laws and consisting of pure bliss. The *caturvarga* and other practical objects of poetry are indeed repeated in unbroken tradition. But when the Sanskrit thinkers put forward a theory of idealised enjoyment, which they regard to be the sole object of poetry, they undoubtedly accept, even from a limited point of view, pure theoretic contemplation as its essence.

This blissful condition reproduced in the reader by the idealised creation of poetry is given as almost equivalent to the philosophical *ānanda*. In explaining that it affords an escape from the natural world by replacing it with an imaginative world, Sanskrit theorists rightly emphasise that, even from the reader's point of view, the function of art is that of the deliverer. What is said of the reader is also true of the poet, for the reader only reproduces what the poet has produced. The crude emotion or impression forms the rich material which the poet absorbs into his psychic organism, but as he passes from these troublous elements, which may be pleasurable or painful, to the blissful serenity of contemplation, he thereby dominates them and frees himself from their tyranny. By the purity of his expressive activity he delivers and purifies himself from the bondage of crude passivity.

In view of the spiritual character of the poetic activity, the question of personality is of the utmost importance in any theory of poetry. In fact, this is the most vital and indispensable problem in treating with aesthetic expression.

It is a matter of ordinary experience, and therefore does not require much research to prove, that what appeals to us in a poem, unless we are obtuse or impervious, is the personality which reveals itself in the warmth, movement, and integrity of imagination and expression. The poet may astonish us with his wealth of facts and thought, or with his cleverness in the manipulation of the language; but this is not what we really ask of a poet. What we want is the expression of a soul, in contact with which our souls may be moved. Some people are indeed interested in profound thought or ethical nobility and want to find them in a work of art; but these are extrinsic intellectual or ethical valuations which have nothing to do with its intrinsic artistic appeal. The personality may be cheerful or melancholy, thoughtful or emotional, serene or perplexed, benignant or malignant; but if it is really a personality, it is sure to arrest and enliven us, apart from every other secondary consideration. Such a personality by itself justifies a work of art, and we never call it dull, cold, or flat. On the other hand, if personality is wanting, all the learning or moralising in the world cannot save a work from artistic failure. For, what does failure mean in a work of art but want of integrity or unity? It means that one powerful and homogeneous personality does not emerge, but a series of disjointed and straggling personalities; synthetic coherence required for successful expression is lacking.

Let it be clearly understood that this spontaneous and ideal personality in a poetical work is not identical with the empirical and volitional personality of the poet. The latter does very often invade or obscure the former, and leave extraneous and undesirable traces of crude and factitious effects. A poet who is unable to attain a proper expression of his true personality is, therefore, often found padding out his work with declamatory or theatrical effects to make up the deficiency. If his practical or intellectual tendencies prevail, he will try to overwhelm by didactic moralisings or richness of thought and facts.

In the case of the critic, too, when his artistic personality does not find free scope, his power of reproduction and appreciation is eclipsed, and his criticism is no longer dispassionate, but prejudiced. One kind of personality, the poetic, which has its proper sphere in this case, is opposed, mastered, or denied by another, which is entirely alien. Theorists who deny the claim of personality and declare that art should be impersonal do not really offer an opposition. When they object that bad artists leave traces of their personality and good artists do not, they only mean to say what we have said about the real artistic personality being fettered or free. Even the strongest advocate of impersonality will admit that the author of a work consisting merely of an industrious compilation of facts and having no trace of personality may be a useful or methodical pedagogue but is no artist.

What is emphasised by the requirement of personality in a work of art is unity. This is not the haphazard unity of diverse kinds of personality, but the intrinsic unity of the work as synthetic expression of one artistic personality. Everyone recognises that the expression alone makes the poet, but not everyone realises that the expression in each case is unique, intrinsic, and indivisible. There is thus no question of outward and inward, real and unreal. From this point of view, the much discussed and variously distinguished terms, like subjective and objective, ideal and real, romantic and classic, lyric, epic, and dramatic, in spite of their usefulness as artifices of empirical classification lose all their force in aesthetic criticism. In the unity of expression the distinctions are not absolute but only indicate moments of representation, and no artistic work can be exclusively this or that. It follows also that if personality is indispensable in a work of art, each work is a concrete, individual, expressive fact of that personality under a specific group of stimuli as well as under definite conditions of time and place. In this sense, all critical appreciation, like all translation of artistic works, is only relative; for the personality of the critic or the translator is very seldom identical with that of the poet, and can hardly reproduce the same intuition under its own conditions of production.

One of the greatest limitations of Sanskrit poetics which hindered its growth into a proper aesthetic was its almost total disinterest in the poetic personality by which a work of art attains its particular shape and individual character. Thereby it neglects a most vital aspect of its task, the study of poetry as the individualised expression of the poet's soul, which should have been one of its fundamental issues. We have scattered glimpses of the fact that the Sanskrit theorists were aware of this supreme problem, but they either regarded it to be outside their scope or did not attack it in its entirety. From this spring most of the deficiencies of their theories.

Sanskrit poetics cannot, for example, explain satisfactorily the simple question of why the work of one poet is not the same in character as that of another, or even why two works of the same poet are not the same. To Sanskrit theorists a composition is a work of art if it fulfils the prescribed requirements of 'qualities', of 'ornaments', of arrangement of words with a view to suggest a sense which is not directly expressed. It is immaterial whether the work in question is the *Raghuvaṃśa** or the *Naiṣadha*.* The main differences theorists will probably observe between these two works will consist of the formal employment of this or that mode of diction, or in their respective skill of suggesting this or that meaning of the words. They never bother themselves about the poetic imagination which gave each a distinct and unique shape in a fusion of impressions into an organic whole. They fail to understand that this is what distinguishes the *Raghuvaṃśa* as a poem from the *Naiṣadha*, as well as from the *Kumārasaṃbhava*.* Their appreciation of the particular power of individual poetic intuition or personality in each case is forgotten in the consideration of universal standards of more-or-less normative requirements. Having destroyed the concrete particular, they prescribed the abstract universal, somewhat in the manner of recommending one measurement for all feet, one garment for all bodies.

It is not surprising, therefore, that we search in vain for a complete definition or clear discussion of the poetic imagination in the whole range of Sanskrit poetics. The theorists, albeit solemnly affirming the necessity of *pratibhā* (imagination) in the poet, in their theories themselves fail to give the *pratibhā* any important or essential role except in a few isolated instances. Vāmana formulises that in *pratibhā* lies the seed of poetry. He describes it as a particular antenatal instinct without which poetry is impossible and its attempt only ridiculous. This empirical observation, however, neither clearly determines its character nor tells us anything about its function. Abhinavagupta perhaps shows more discernment when he explains it as an intuition (*prajñā*) capable of ever fresh invention, its distinguishing sphere being the power of creating absorption in *rasa*, clarity, beauty, and poetry. He further quotes the authority of Bharata, who designates it as the internal emotion (*antargatabhāva*) of the poet.* These tentative descriptions indicate that the theorists vaguely recognised the necessity of poetic imagination, but failed to assign an adequate role to it in their normative schemes.

The failure to explain and justify poetry by the poetic imagination is indeed a serious gap which has led the Sanskrit authors into theoretic difficulties and perplexities. Bhāmaha, for instance, and following him Kuntaka, reject the figuré *svabhāvokti* on the ground that it consists of mere unadorned description of physical objects. But the poetic intuition of a physical fact, even if unadorned, is not the same as a matter-of-fact statement or description, and Daṇḍin and others rightly take it into account. Both Bhāmaha and Daṇḍin betray an uneasiness over the character of the figure *bhāvika*,* not knowing whether to classify it as 'quality' * or 'ornament'. We have seen that Kuntaka made an important contribution when he spoke of a kind of expression other than those which predicate empirical facts or logical relations, and posed the problem definitely for the first time by emphasising the function of the poetic imagination. But we also saw that he could not develop a complete theory of poetic production on the basis of what he had only dimly seen. His *kavikarman* limited itself mainly to a normative analysis of empirical canons, and made his poetics assume, as usual, a verbal and formal character, in which his fundamental suggestion was lost. His contribution, therefore, remained a hazy sketch which never attracted notice and which was never completed.

The orthodox theorists, on the other hand, attempted to comprehend all they had to say about poetic imagination in their theory of *rasa*. But they consider the problem indirectly and imperfectly from the standpoint of the reader, and not directly and completely from that of the poet. As we have said above, they are concerned mainly with the question of the reader's reproduction but not of the poet's production. The two aspects of the question are indeed fundamentally the same, and thereby they undoubtedly had a correct idea of the problem. But this inverse process was never pushed further and did not enable them to reach the ultimate goal. Their restricted angle of approach made them concern themselves with abstract concepts within whose formal circle their vision was caught and entrammelled. They could not free themselves from the starting barrier of regarding words as fixed and mechanical symbols, from splitting up the concrete unity of synthetic poetic expression into an abstract dualism of exteriority and interiority. The distinction between the unexpressed and the expressed, like that between the simple and the ornate, is only a logical and not an aesthetic distinction. The same poetic intuition expresses itself in one and one way only, precisely because it is a concrete intuition and not an abstract concept. The question of distinction, therefore, does not arise, except for logical exposition.

The same tendency to abstraction betrays itself in their theory of idealised enjoyment in the reader, which they present, more or less, as an abstract enjoyment of abstract symbols. They hardly realise that aesthetically Rāma whom the poet represents is always Rāma, and never a mere force or abstraction.* The poet never leaves the concrete, even if he has an idealised image of it. Hence come the appealing warmth and life of his creation, which is indeed enjoyed by us ideally in the form of his serene contemplation, but which is nevertheless vividly real. The old psychology knew something about the poetic intuition, but its productive activity, which is autonomous in relation to abstract concepts given by the intellectual function, was imperfectly understood.

This imperfect understanding of the function of the imagination is also shown by the whole discussion on the so-called 'objects' of poetry, as well as by the vacillation and uncertainty which we find in the various attempts to discover a rigid definition of poetry. Since the expressive activity is a purely spiritual necessity, this alone, theoretically speaking, can be its absolute object. Other 'objects' —knowledge, pleasure, virtue—are only relative, having certain practical or intellectual application, which is entirely extrinsic. There is, therefore, an element of truth in the common saying that a poet speaks because he must speak, just as a man possessing a strong will cannot help realising it in action. The failure clearly and explicitly to understand the nature of poetic intuition, which differs in different poets, led many a Sanskrit theorist to attempt many a cut-and-dried definition of poetry. They made vain efforts to find one abstract and universal formula for what admits of infinite individual and concrete variations; to determine logically what in its essence is non-logical; to immobilise the mobile by throwing a bridle on the neck of Pegasus.

Similar imperfect understanding is also shown by what the Sanskrit theorists often say about culture (*vyutpatti*) and practice (*abhyāsa*) in relation to the poetic imagination (*pratibhā*). To be sure, the fact of poetic representation is preceded by various kinds of knowledge which, like feelings or physical facts, act as a stimulus or material. As adventitious aids to externalisation they have a certain relative value. In so far as this is acknowledged, the Sanskrit theorists justly remark that culture and practice should assist poetic power. But, protesting their belief in the poetic imagination, they sometimes go further and speak of "making a poet into a poet." Rudraṭa, for instance, expresses his opinion that the poetic imagination is not only inborn but also capable of attainment by culture. The poet is thus required to be an expert in a long list of disciplines, such as grammar, lexicon, metrics, arts, scriptures, legends, law, logic, philosophy, morals, erotics, dramaturgy, poetics, politics, and even such miscellaneous subjects as medicine, botany, astronomy, magic, science of archery and military operations, elephant lore, veterinary science, art of gambling, and knowledge of precious stones. It is also prescribed that the poet should make himself proficient in poetical exercise. He must be clever at weaving metaphors and other figures, at the trick of producing a double meaning, at manipulating complicated schemes of alliteration, assonance, and rhyming, at following up quick composition, at making complete strophes out of broken lines and sentences, and similar skilful practices. This demand was in conformity with the learned atmosphere in which poetry at one time came to flourish and which made poetics assume a scholastic character. In actual practice, no doubt, the gifted poets aspired to untrammelled utterance; but the general tendency in an epoch of relative decadence in culture degenerated towards a slavish adherence to rules, which obscured and dominated the intuitive activity, and which naturally resulted in the overloading of a composition with artificial devices.

Hence we have a group of rhetoricians who deal with the theme of *kaviśikṣā* (education of the poet) and furnish elaborate instructions to the aspiring poet in the artifices of his craft.* The theory thus believes in a doctrine of technique, in the teaching of the means of poetic intuition or expression. It is curious indeed that this practical object developed side by side with theoretic considerations. As is commonly remarked, however, no amount of profound culture or technical skill can make a poet. Since poetic expression is a theoretic activity, it is independent of the secondary practical activity, as well as of intellectual knowledge, both of which do not illuminate it but are illuminated by it. As it consists of pure intuition of things, it has nothing to do with volitional effort about which we speak of means and end. If we say that a poet has a new technique, we really mean to imply that the new technique is the poem itself. A poetic intuition cannot have a prescribed technique of expression, for the simple reason that it is an intuition, of which the expression is merely the actuality. It is not an intellectual concept which can be logically or universally formulated. Nor is there any passage to it from the physical fact or the intellectual concept. It stands by itself.

We come again, then, to the point that the poetic intuition differs in each poet, according to his psychic organism and the nature of the stimuli acting upon it, and there are bound, therefore, to be endless kinds of individual and concrete expression which have their own standards and spheres in each case, and which cannot repeat themselves. The technique of the poet is his poetic conception itself; it may be a failure or a success, but there cannot be, theoretically speaking, any question of good, bad, or indifferent technique. Even the ordinary man, therefore, never believes in the manufacturing of ready-made poetry. The enumeration of useful sciences or the collection of technical knowledge can never be exhausted by formal treatment. It may serve the practical purpose of supplying information about material or groups of stimuli, or even the logical purpose of exposition, but it possesses no theoretic value for the fact of poetic creation.

The same inability to understand fully the essential character of the poetic imagination or expression is responsible for the zeal with which the theorists devote themselves to collect, analyse, and classify methodically, after the manner of natural sciences, a series of single facts into universal formulas and categories. Such an empirical attitude admits indeed the existence of occurrences called aesthetic or artistic, but nourishes a delusion that they can be grouped formally into broad classes and types. In the course of their investigation they amass, calculate, and measure the greatest possible variety of such facts, formulate laws, means, modes, and models. But as they progress they always discover new facts, which require fresh adjustment. Here, too, they indicate failure to realise that each expression is unique and indivisible; that artistic facts in their unified concreteness cannot, like physical facts, be divided and subdivided; that they cannot, like intellectual facts, be logically formulated into abstract universals. They forget that a work of art is an intuition, that intuition is individuality, and that individuality never repeats itself nor conforms to a prescribed mould. They believe, thus, not in the unity but in the duality of imagination and expression, thereby splitting up what is organic into mechanic parts. It is hardly recognised that words, as symbols, are inseparable from intuition, that they are not fixed but mobile, not an embalmed collection of dead abstractions, but an ever elusive series of living particulars. An empirical technique of what is free and theoretical is a contradiction in terms.

Sanskrit poetics inherited this tendency from Sanskrit grammar,* which in its normative character always proved a bar to understanding the nature of expression. Some of the piteous perplexities of Sanskrit poetics are, thus, intelligible. Good sense has always refused to accept a normative formulation of poetic expression, whether grammatical or aesthetic. Only the poor or, at best, indifferent speaker or versifier speaks or writes by rules; merely following cut-and-dried rules never leads to speaking or writing well. For the real poet, as for the real speaker, there is hardly any armoury of ready-made weapons; he forges his own weapons to fight his own particular battles.

Let it not be supposed that we wish to deny or minimise the usefulness of such analysis and classification from the scientific or scholastic point of view. What we want to stress is that they fail to establish their claim to explain the energies of the intuitive activity of poetic creation. Such distinctions as are industriously presented in these works are made by reflective consciousness; they are not essential to the fact itself. As logical concepts or natural facts they are admissible and are of practical assistance, but they have hardly any theoretical importance. They are like labels attached to a thing, and not the thing itself. Their elaboration *as laws* constitutes, in effect, a negation of art itself. By their presumption of universality, they negate its accidentality; by their abstraction, its empiricity; by their mechanism, its organic character.

Thus, Sanskrit poetics, purportedly engaged in solving

the poetic riddle, delighted, rather, in the pleasure of abstract thought and formal calculation. Its method is suitable for the study of botany or zoology, but affords hardly any assistance for the understanding of aesthetic facts or principles. While it had an intuitive realisation of the true nature of poetry, it confined its intellectual prepossession to the formulation of pedagogic expedients or normative abstractions. Nevertheless, the aberrations are at the same time attempts to reach the truth; and in the midst of unlifted shadows one does often perceive a running thread of silver lining.

NOTES

by Edwin Gerow

(Notes are keyed by page and line of this volume; e.g., 1.1
refers to page 1, line 1 of the text. Within the notes, references
such as 2.22 refer to section 2, verse or sūtra 22; those such as
7/38 refer to page 7, line 38.)

NOTES TO CHAPTER 1. INTRODUCTION

1.1 kāvya: In general 'the literary product', from *kavi*,
originally 'seer' but in later and classical Sanskrit
the usual word for 'poet'. *Kāvya*, in the sense of
'literature' is common to both prose and poetry,
though it is often translated by 'poetry'. By syn-
ecdoche it is often taken to signify the "great"
literary works, sometimes enumerated at six:
lengthy epics in elevated style and complicated
metre, such as the *Raghuvaṃśa* and *Kumārasa-
mbhava* of Kālidāsa.

1.3 ādi-śloka: The 'first verse'; Vālmīki, the traditional
author of the *Rāmāyaṇa*, is said to have spontaneously produced the first metrical utterance, and
thus is considered the discoverer of poetry. See-
ing the female of a pair of *krauñcas* ('curlews')
bereaved at the loss of her mate to the senseless
arrow of a hunter, Vālmīki said to the hunter *"mā
niṣāda pratiṣṭhāṃ tvam agamaḥ śāśvatīḥ samāḥ
/ yat krauñcamithunād ekam avadhīḥ kāmamohi-
tam"* (*Rāmāyaṇa* 2.15) "may you not rest forever-
more, for you have killed this curlew distraught
with love." This happens to be a śloka, one of the
simplest metres, and serves as a pretext for a
pun, as Vālimīki is said to have turned his sorrow
(*śoka*) into verse (*śloka*). (*Dhvanyāloka* 1.5.)

1.5 *mayā: Rāmāyaṇa* 2.16.

1.16 grammar: Skt. *vyākaraṇa*. The most authoritative of
the scholastic disciplines, which has served as a
model for much erudite speculation. Grammatical
teaching was codified by Pāṇini (*ca.* 400 B.C.), and
his treatment, which is formal, symbolic, and systematic (much in the style of the present day),
had probably become canonical by the early form-
ative period of poetics (A.D. 200–600) and may

have contributed to the alleged aridity of some Indian speculation.

1.24   *vidvāmsah:* Ā on Dhv. p. 47/1.2; *infra* page 8.

1.28   Vāmana: Bhām. ch. 6; Vāmana. ch. 5.

1.29   Panini: Bhām. 6.62–3; for these writers, see notes 2.35 and 5.4.

2.29   *kuta idam:* 'what', not 'how' or 'whence'.

2.34   embellishment: The word *alamkāra*, lit. 'ornament', from *alam* 'sufficient', 'able', and *kṛ-* 'making'. The etymology thus betrays the religious or magical function originally attributed to 'embellishment': that which gives sufficiency or power to common, unsanctified, and unadorned speech. The word however soon takes on the connotations of the English 'ornament'—extrinsic decoration—and it is generally in this sense that *alamkāra* is applied to the poetic figures of speech. The science of poetics, having begun in speculation on these *alamkāras*, is usually referred to as *alamkāraśāstra*, even though many later theorists ignored or belittled the 'figures'.

2.35   Rudraṭa: With Udbhaṭa, the three foremost writers of the *alamkāra* school. Bhāmaha, who probably wrote towards the end of the seventh century, may have engaged in a controversy with Daṇḍin (*infra* page 5) over the importance of style in poetry. Because he rejects the notion and concerns himself primarily with figures of speech, he is assigned to the *alamkāra* school in the narrow sense. Rudraṭa (ninth century) is more eclectic, but his treatment of *alamkāra* so far outweighs in pure mass his account of style that he is put also in the school. See note 5.4 and Chapter II.

3.10   specialists: *Ca.* A.D. 700–900. The works of Māgha and Śrīharṣa are a case in point: though classified among the great poems by Indian critics, most Western authorities consider them overly ornate, devoid of originality, and based for their appeal on an exploitation of the grammatical pyrotechnics of the Sanskrit language. See *infra* page 72.

3.23   *ālamkārika:* Agent noun: one who concerns himself with *alamkāra;* in the widest sense, 'poetician'.

4.6   *vakrokti:* Lit. 'indirect speech'; *infra* page 34 and Chapter III.

4.9   ornaments: Bhām. 2.81, 85.

4.9   Udbhaṭa: End of eighth century. His perhaps fragmentary work, the *Kāvyālamkārasārasamgraha,* treats of nothing but the figures, and repeats Bhāmaha frequently, hence his assignment to the *alaṃkāra* school.

4.31 Bharata: the probably legendary figure to which the *Nāṭyaśāstra* (*Treatise on Dramaturgy*) is ascribed. This work, the earliest known speculation on the "fine arts", though containing much of an earlier date, was compiled in its present form about the sixth century A.D. It treats of certain ancillary subjects, such as mood and sentiment, and it enumerates four *alaṃkāra*: simile, metaphor, zeugma, and homophony. The next writer, Bhāmaha (seventh century), is the first to base his work on an examination of the figures, and he enumerates more than 40. Bharata is thus the "uncle" rather than the "father" of *alaṃkāraśāstra*.

4.31 Jayadeva: A fourteenth-century writer whose *Candrāloka* is considered today by many pundits the standard treatise on the figures of speech. Although more than 100 individual figures are enumerated, many of them are nothing but elaborations of subsidiary distinctions already proposed in earlier writers.

5.4 *rīti*: Lit. 'style'. The history of poetic speculation (*alaṃkāraśāstra*) is commonly treated in terms of several "schools," which had a roughly but not absolutely chronological vogue. The oldest is called simply the *alaṃkāra* school from its preoccupation with the figures (*supra* page 2). The second of the schools is usually characterized as the *rīti*, from the place of honor it gives to this stylistic idea. Daṇḍin (first half of the eighth century) and Vāmana (*ca.* A.D. 800) were the proponents of this literary movement. Subsequent schools emphasized *rasa* 'mood' and *dhvani* 'suggestion'. In none of the later schools were the figures rejected, though their relative importance was questioned. Daṇḍin, for example, though generally considered an exponent of the *rīti* school, gives the most exhaustive treatment of the figures known in the period before 1000. The problem of the schools is complicated by difficulties of chronology, not the least of which is an argument as to whether Daṇḍin actually did follow Bhāmaha, which seems to be an essential postulate of the "developmental" aspect of the school theory. The authors engage in a remarkable amount of mutual refutation. In any case, the *alaṃkāra* school enjoyed sustained popularity, as evidenced by the works of Rudraṭa (ninth century) and Ruyyaka (mid-twelfth century).

5.5 words: Vām. 1.2.6, 7.

5.9 poetry: Daṇ. 2.1.

5.11 sense: Daṇ. 2.3.

5.13 speech: Vām. 3.1.2, 3.

5.15 *guṇas:* One of the most important items in the philosophical vocabulary of Sanskrit; lit. 'chord', 'string', from this 'subdivision' or 'aspect', finally 'property', 'virtue'. In this last and now primary use, the word carries the same ambiguity as English 'quality': neutral, as in " 'audibility' is a quality of sound" and mejorative, as in "among his qualities were steadfastness and truthfulness". In poetic speculation, the word *guṇa* denotes ten properties of poetic utterance which permit the discrimination of different *rīti,* and differ from the figures in referring more to utterance and composition than to form and content.

5.17 forth: The ten *guṇas* of Daṇḍin and Vāmana are *śleṣa* (coherence of long sentences without hiatus or grammatical breaks), *prasāda* (simplicity), *samatā* (uniformity in the type of consonant cluster used), *mādhurya* (highly emotive speech), *sukumaratā* (predominance of liquid consonants), *arthavyakti* (clarity), *udāratva* (nobility of subject), *ojas* (use of long compound words), *kānti* (agreeable commonplaces), and *samādhi* (metaphorical speech in general). Daṇ. 1.41 ff, Vām. 3.1.5 ff. The various styles (*rīti*) are distinguished as they employ one or several of these qualities or their contraries, which are also presumably "qualities", though of a more equivocal character.

5.21 modes: Daṇ. 2.3.

5.24 qualities: Vām. 3.1.2, 3.

5.29 produced: Cf. Mammaṭa, *Kāvyaprakāśa,* 1.3.

6.1 individuality: Rather in the sense of the "renaissance" style. *Infra.* page 7.

6.12 *doṣas:* From the verb *duṣ*—'become corrupt'. A moral "flaw" is also called a *doṣa.* "Defect" is a secondary topic of all the *alaṃkāra* writers except Udbhaṭa, and the concept has like that of figure been extensively subdivided. *Guṇa* and *doṣa,* like their English counterparts 'virtue' and 'vice', always seem to attract one another in any theory, but the parallelism in Sanskrit aesthetics is a bit skew: in the later writers the "flaws" are paired more with the "figures" (lit. 'ornaments') rather than with the "qualities", as the latter disappear or become vestigial. The present discussion concerns only early usage and its origins.

6.29 poetic intuition: It should be made clear at the outset that Professor De's point of view is contemporary and Western, and that he is criticising Sanskrit aesthetics from that point of view. His use of terms such as "poetic intuition" does not imply that such ideas were of importance in the Indian tradition, or were there felt to be necessary as principles of poetic investigation. Indeed it is apparent from the literature that such is not always the case; Professor De is attempting creatively to unite or transcend the two (Western and Indian) traditions, rather than simply to portray philologically the Indian tradition. This will be made clearer in Chapter V.

7.9 spirit: See previous note.

7.19 expression: Most early writers on *alaṃkāra* make the same observation, and do not carry the analysis beyond what is felt to be the level of poetic relevance. Bhām. 2.38, Daṇ. 1.40, 1.104, 2.1. Dhv. 1.7, 2.13. Later writers in some cases appear to claim exhaustive treatment of the subject. Rud. 7.9, 10.24.

7.34 other: Daṇ. 1.40. *Vaidarbhī* and *Gauḍī* are adjectives corresponding to Vidarbha and Gauḍa—modern Berar and Bengal.

7.35 *Pāñcālī*. Vām. 1.2.9 (*Pāñcālī* from Pañcāla—modern Oudh).

7.36 qualities: Vām. 1.2.11.

7.37 *Lāṭī:* AP 340.1. Rud. 2.4. *Lāṭiyā*, also derived from the name of a region (modern Gujerat), occurs more often as the name of a kind of alliteration (Bhām. 2.8, Ud. 1.8, Mam. 112), also as a *Prākṛta* (Daṇ. 1.35).

7.37 *Āvantikā* and *Māgadhī:* BSP (unpublished).

8.13 word and sense: Dhv. 1.7. The *dhvani* school, by which is generally understood three writers: an anonymous *"Dhvanikāra"* (8th century), his commentator Ānandavardhana (9th century), and his (Ānandavardhana's) commentator Abhinavagupta (9th–10th). The first two together constitute the text of the canonical *Dhvanyāloka*.

8.17   denotation: In Sanskrit *abhidhā* or *abhidhāna* (name).

8.17   indication: *Lakṣaṇa* ('sign', 'token').

8.19   allied sense: For example, the literal sense of the word 'grandstand' is the well-known object constructed of metal and wood, but in the phrase "the grandstands are yelling" it cannot have that sense, since, for one reason, grandstands are incapable of uttering sound. Hence the secondary or "indicated" meaning (whereof the literal word is a "token") is "those who people the grandstands". Cf. Dhv. 1.4 and commentary and Mam. ch. 5.

8.23   suggestion: Skt. "*vyañjanā*" from the root *vyaj*—'manifesting'. The poetry based on suggestion is called commonly *dhvani* ('intimation').

8.26   indicated sense: The mark of suggested meaning is that it is neither the literal meaning (*abhidhā*) nor is it incompatible with the literal meaning (as *lakṣaṇa*), but it must be founded on either one or the other, since the suggestion meant is that of verbal expression, not that of gestures, non-linguistic utterance, and the like. For example, the idea of evil can be suggested either through the "literal" phrase "Mephistopheles walks among the souls of the dead" or through the "token" words: "The virtuous Mephistopheles decries the vices of mankind", where neither 'virtuous' nor 'vices' can be taken literally. In the latter case the idea of evil, though founded on the secondary meaning, is not incompatible with it, and is not therefore a "secondary" secondary meaning. The consideration of these three meanings in their poetic implications, and especially of the third (suggestion) in relation to the generalized mood (*rasa*) of the work of art, constitutes the major topic of the third "school" of poetic theory, the *dhvani* school.

8.29   *vyaṅgya*: The discussion of the three "meanings" is greatly facilitated by three analogous trilogies of referents, the rendition of which into English is cumbrous in the extreme, but which exemplify the elegance and the finesse of the derivational process in Sanskrit: 1(a) *abhidhā* or *vācaka* (word expressing the literal meaning), (b) *abhidheya* or *vācya* (literal meaning to be expressed), (c) *abhidhānā* or *vācanā* (literal signification); 2(a) *lākṣaṇika* (word expressing the secondary meaning), (b) *lakṣya* (secondary meaning to be expressed), (c) *lakṣaṇā* (secondary signification); and 3(a) *vyañjaka* (word expressing the suggested meaning), (b) *vyaṅgya* (meaning to be suggested), (c) *vyañjanā* (suggestion). Mam. 5, 6, 11, 12, 22; Dhv. 1.2.

8.32 essence: *"Vyaṅgya"* is not posited as category of being, but only as an end corresponding to a formally distinguishable means: the *vyañjaka*, or suggestive word(s). Thus it has only a relational or functional existence.

8.37 utterance: Dhv. 1.14, 3.37.

9.19 unexpressed sentiment: *Infra* page 49 and note 49.12.

9.26 poetry: Dhv. 1.1.

10.7 semantic: Bhām. 6.1 et seq.; Vām. 5.2.1 et seq.; Mam. 72 (example 142) (the defect [*doṣa*] *cyutasaṃskṛti* or 'fallen Sanskrit' and following "defects").

10.12 purpose: I.e., when the "unexpressed" predominates in a poem it *is* the "purpose." Mam. 7.

10.25 opinion: The *dhvani* or "suggestion" school.

10.33 "agreeable language": Ā on Dhv. 1.1., p. 5/1 ff.; Bhām. 1.16; Daṇ. 1.18–19.

10.33 emotion: Skt. *bhāva;* the problem of the emotions was central in the speculations of Bharata on the drama (NŚ 6.38), and thus predates strictly speaking the birth of *alaṃkāra* (see note 4.31). But it forms an important theme parallel to and within the history of *alaṃkāra*, and those writers who give more emphasis to the aspect of emotion are sometimes deemed to constitute the fourth "school" of poetics. (See Chapter IV, and note 11.15.) The *dhvani* theorists, while recognizing emotion as the central problem of aesthetics, treat is as a case (the crucial case) of *vyaṅgya* (note 8.29). Thus the emphasis remains on suggestion, even though at first glance the *dhvani* theory may appear to concentrate on emotion. The following discussion relates to the "third" school, specifically to their criticism and evaluation of the topics advanced by this "fourth" school (herein unnamed).

10.37 theorists: *Dhvani* theorists.

11.2 suggest it: Cf. Ā on Dhv. p. 25/1 ff.

11.9 receptacle: NŚ 6.33; cf. Bharata's account of the eight *rasas*, in which these aspects are set forth.

11.12 poetry: Abh. on NŚ, p. 284/8–10.

11.15 relish: Skt. *rasa* is not the physical and immediate emotion whose portrayal is always particular (*bhāva*), but the generalized resultant "emotion"

in the spectator, which is shared by all the specta-
tors and in principle by all men. This distinction
is the subject of the following discussion and is
taken up again in Chapter IV. Attempts have
generally been made to render *"rasa"* in English
by calling it 'relish', 'taste', 'mood', and so on.
Etymologically this is justified, as *rasa* derives
from a root *ras-* 'tasting', in the literal sense (cf.
rasanā, 'tongue'). The phrase "relish of the emotions" must be understood as "rising to the occasion of the matter" or "delectation of (the spirit
of) a particular crisis." SKD *HSP* vol. 2, p. 35. It
is well to emphasize however that the Sanskrit
theorists do not express themselves in this way, as
though the problem were to generate or explain
the *rasa* in the spectator starting from the portrayal of the *bhāva* (emotion); rather the rasa is
taken as principle, and the problem is to explain
the nature of the representation and its capacity
to "enliven" the *rasa*. Bhaṭṭa Nāyaka says
". . . *bhāvyamāno rasaḥ*", 'the rasa is to be en-
livened . . . (by means of situations, gestures,
etc.)'. Abh. on NŚ 277/3.

11.18   felt: Abh. on NŚ p. 275/10 ff.; Abh. cited by KPK p.
97/11 ff.

11.22   emotion: Abh. cited by KPK p. 96/10 ff.

11.25   sense: NŚ, 6.34–8; Dhv. 1.8.

11.30   factors: The "means of expression" are traditionally
classified into *vibhāva* (conditions appropriate to
the emotion to be expressed, as a garden or a
beautiful woman), *anubhāva* (consequents and
exterior manifestations of the emotion, by which
it is communicated, as sidelong glances, fondling),
vyabhicāribhāva (temporary states which accom-
pany emotions but suggest in themselves no *rasa*
and produce no *vāsanā*, as languor, irritation, etc.
Cf. Abh. on NŚ p. 283/3–7), and *sāttvikabhāva*
(physical and involuntary "products", as hor-
ripilation, sweating, fainting, etc.)

11.31   causes: Opinion attributed to Bhaṭṭa Lollata by Abh.
on NŚ p. 272/4. His work is now lost. Bhaṭṭa
Lollata asserted that the *vibhāvas* accompanied by
an appropriate selection of the other types "cause"
the rasa in the spectator. See preceding note.

11.34   case: Abh. on NŚ p. 272/16 (citing Srīśaṅkuka), p.
285/2; VSD 3.37.

11.38   *rasa:* Abh. on NŚ p. 279/13–14. On "impressions"
        (*vāsanā*) see *infra,* page 12; VSD 3.40.
12.3   separately: Dhv. 1.12; Abh. on NŚ 279/3–6; Abh.
        by KPK p. 99/9–10.
12.4   indivisible: Abh. on NŚ p. 279/14; VSD 3.46.
12.5   obliterated: Abh. cited by KPK p. 102/8–9; VSD
        3.47, 54.
12.8   *vāsanā:* From a root *vas-* 'dwell'; in its most general
        meaning *vāsanā* signifies 'potential memory', that
        is, that subconscious unity which underlies spe-
        cific remembrances of a given thing (actual mem-
        ory). As such *vāsanā* is a key concept in the psy-
        chologies of saṃsara and rebirth, and is taken by
        Śaṃkara as a principle explaining (erroneous)
        impressions, specifically those based on the sup-
        posed unity of soul and body (Ego). In *rasa* the-
        ory, as seen by Abhinavagupta, the term can be
        taken as the ground of passage from the appre-
        hension of the specific representation to the gen-
        eral appreciation of it.
12.9   instincts: VSD 3.39.
12.10   suggested: Abh. on NŚ p. 284/9 *"prācyakāraṇādi-*
        rūpasaṃskāropajīvanakhyāpanā".
12.13   poetry: Abh. on NŚ p. 284/7; VSD 3.37; *laukika/*
        alaukika ('common'/'uncommon') from *loka* 'the
        people, vulgus'.
12.15   particularities: VSD 3.40 cf. Abh. on NŚ p. 279/5–6.
12.17   beloved: VSD 3.42; Abh. on Dhv. 2.4, p. 69/3–7; cf.
        DDR 4.41; JRGĀ pp. 42 passim.
12.19   love in general: VSD 3.43.
12.24   readers in general: Abh. on NŚ p. 279/13–14 *sarva-*
        sāmājikānām ekaghanatayaiva pratipattiḥ sutarāṃ
        rasaparitoṣāya. Also, Abh. on NŚ p. 280/8.
12.28   sensibility: the *sahṛdaya,* the ideal audience and the
        proper poetic context. Of this more later (page
        54).
12.29   *sādhāraṇīkaraṇa:* VSD 3.40; from *sādhāraṇa* 'having
        a common substratum' and *karaṇa* 'making, ef-
        fecting'. The translation 'generalization' should be
        understood in the sense of 'broadening', not ab-
        stracting'. (Abh. on NŚ p. 279/10.) The emo-
        tional and affective aspect is not left behind, but
        rather a new kind of emotion is experienced,
        which is essentially shared. Abh. by KPK p. 97/13.
        This doctrine apparently was taken over from
        Bhaṭṭa Nāyaka by Abhinavagupta: Abh. by KPK
        p. 95/10 on *"bhāvakatvam".*

12.35 others: Dhv. 1.4; Abh. on Dhv. p. 14/12–13.
12.37 sense: VSD 3.35–6.
 13.2 joy: *"Ānanda"*.
 13.3 by itself: Abh. on NŚ p. 285/3-4.
 13.8 relish itself: Abh. on NŚ p. 284/11 (*carvyamāṇatai-
 kasāraḥ*).
13.12 *brahmāsvāda*: Abh. on NŚ p. 277/4 (referring to
 Bhaṭṭanāyaka); Abh. by KPK p. 99/8; Mam. p.
 99/3; VSD 3.34, etc. Cf. note 12.29.
13.14 permanent: Abh. on NŚ p. 284/11–12; JRGĀ p.
 39/11.
13.18 *viśrānti*: Not only is *viśrānti* the result of the aesthetic experience, but it is one of the tests of its
 success, inasmuch as the mind which has not been
 able to pass beyond the contemplation of particular events and emotions is necessarily "obstructed"
 by its participation in them. The *rasa* is imperfectly realized. Abh. on NŚ p. 280/8, 14 ff.
13.20 place: Abh. on NŚ p. 284/7–10.
13.22 *citsvabhāvā saṃvit*. Cf. S. K. De, HSP vol. ii p. 137
 footnote.
13.26 proof: Abh. on NŚ p. 284/11 (*na tu siddhasvabhā-
 vah*).
13.28 of itself: Abh. on NŚ p. 284/12 (*tātkālika eva na tu
 carvaṇātiriktakālāvalambī*).
13.31 vouchsafed: VSD 3.57.
13.39 attitude: VSD 3.39; Abh. cited by KPK p. 97/7.
 14.3 *tanmayībhavaṇa yogyatā*: Abh. on Dhv. p. 11/23–4.
 14.9 food: Bharata himself gives the gastronomic analogy: *text* following 6.31.
14.13 Jacobi: Translator of the *Dhvanyāloka* (Leipzig,
 1903).
14.20 feelings: Prabhā on Pradīpa p. 82/23–5.
14.24 accepted: The *bhāvas* (feelings) are generic in the
 sense that all the other factors of composition are
 subordinate to them; among which are the *vyabhicāribhāvas* or specific feelings. See note to 11.30.
 The *bhāvas* also correspond each to a *rasa*.
14.33 obliterated: *Supra* page 12.
14.35 it: Sf. VSD 3.36.
14.35 Viśvanātha: A writer of the first half of the fourteenth century (SKD HSP vol. 1, p. 214) whose
 work the *Sāhityadarpaṇa* is one of the standard
 resumes of poetic theory. Although he decrees
 that the "soul" of poetry is *rasa*, he follows closely
 Mammaṭa (see note 32.18) in an encyclopaedic
 compilation of previously treated categories.
 14.39 enjoyment: VSD 3.38. Cf. *supra* p. 52.

15.1   Jagannātha: Mid-seventeenth century; the last great writer on poetics. He follows rather closely but with great independence of judgment the earlier *dhvani* writers Ānandavardhana and Abhinavagupta; but curiously enough, he devotes three-fourths of his work to defining the figures.

15.3   enjoyment: JRGĀ p. 45/7–10.

15.13   *vāgvikalpāh:* Ā on Dhv. p. 210/5–6.

15.15   categories: Ā on Dhv. p. 210/2–6.

15.18   poet: Ā on Dhv. p. 181/10 ff.; Ā on Dhv. p. 210/6–7.

15.22   *rasa:* Dhv. 3.41; 2.6.

15.26   appropriateness: Ā on Dhv. p. 185/17–18.

15.28   employment: Dhv. chapter 3 *passim,* especially 3.6–9, 32.

15.33   composition: Ā on Dhv. p. 134/10–16.

15.36   meaningless: Ā on Dhv. p. 135/7–8; p. 136/1–2; p. 137/7; p. 138/5–6.

15.37   them: Ā on Dhv. p. 138/6 ff; p. 140.

16.1   mind: Dhv. 2.7–10; VSD 8.608, 611, 613; the three are *ojas* 'vigor' (use of long compounds), *mādhurya* 'affection' (appropriate to love stories), and *prasāda* 'clarity' (which can be used in any context). See *supra* page 5.

16.5   qualities: VSD 8.616 ff.

17.15   fact: Vāmana attempts to define all the non-verbal figures as variations of simile.

17.16   in it: VSD 1.3: "Poetry is speech whose essence is delectation (*rasa*)."

NOTES TO CHAPTER 2. THE PROBLEM OF POETIC EXPRESSION

18.5   *artha:* One of the commonplace distinctions in which Sanskrit erudition abounds; compare French *forme et fond.* Any respectable discipline had to account for it. The primary meaning of *śabda* is derived from the grammatical writers, where the entire apparatus of formal categories goes by this name (Pāṇ. i.1.68) and stands over and against any intentional or semantic power that the "word" may have. *Artha* of course stands for that power, and is a stronger word than the translation 'meaning' may convey, for it implies an aim, an intention, a will (e.g. *arthaśāstra,* the science of the [political] good).

18.7   expressed: See note 8.29.

18.15   Bhāmaha: See notes 4.31, 2.35.

18.16 *kāvyam:* Bhām. 1.16: "*kāvya* is word and meaning combined".

18.16 Rudraṭa: A mid-ninth-century writer commonly ascribed to the *alaṃkāra* school. See note 2.35.

18.17 *śabdārthau kāvyam:* Rud. 2.1: "*kāvya* is word and meaning".

18.18 *padāvalī:* Daṇ. 1.10: "A series of words distinguished by a desired meaning". The "body" of poetry is a literal translation of Daṇḍin's '*śarīram*'; in this *kārikā* he analogizes the substance of a poem and its figures to a body and its ornaments.

18.19 racanā Vām. 1.2.7: "A composition of differentiated ('distinguished') words". What is being defined here is not '*kāvya*' but *rīti* (style), which Vāmana has proposed in the preceding *sūtra* as the "essence" (*ātmā*) of *kāvya*. See note 5.4.

18.22 unity: Lit. 'togetherness' or 'combination'. See note 18.16a. *Sāhitya* became a synonym for *kāvya* (see note 1.1) during the medieval period (*ca.* 1000 and later).

18.25 Kuntaka: *Fl. ca.* A.D. 1000, a contemporary of Abhinavagupta, and one of the rare original minds of later poetics. His work, the *Vakroktijīvita*, falls into none of the accepted "schools", and is an attempt to account for poetry in terms of the *essentially* nonliteral character (*vakrokti:* indirect speech) of its statements. See Chapter III.

18.25 *anyūnānatiriktatva:* Kun. 1.17; 'lacking both insufficiency and excess', that is, in which neither the word nor the sense predominates.

18.26 *parasparaspardhā:* Kun. text on 1.7 (p. 29/8); text on 1.17 (p. 60/5); 'mutual antipathy or rivalry'. This refers to the characteristics of the non-literal expression (as in irony, sarcasm, *double-entendre*) whereby the meanings intended seem to be at variance with the words which express them (taken in their literal garb). This "rivalry" distinguishes the "togetherness" of poetic word and sense from "appropriateness" of scientific usage, for example.

18.29 *artha:* Kālidāsa, *Raghuvaṃsa* 1.1: *vāgarthāv iva saṃpṛktau vāgarthapratipattaye jagataḥ pitarau vande pārvatīparameśvarau.* (Ardhanārīśvara is the form of Siva which is half male, half female.)

19.3 *apekṣate:* Māgha, *Śiśupālavadha* 2.86.

19.20 correctness: See note 1.28.

19.23 *vācyasaṃbandha:* Kun. text on 1.7 (p. 25/8); "connection of expressor and expressed". See note 8.29.

19.27 *Pramāṇa: pada:* 'word', vākya: 'sentence' (n.b.: not *vācya*); *pramāṇa*: 'criterion'; in logic the various sources of knowledge, as perception, inference, etc., are called *pramāṇas*. Kun. text on 1.17 (p. 62/5 ff.).

19.37 *Ābhyantara*: *bāhya*: 'exterior', 'external'; *ābhyantara*: 'interior', 'essential' The *dhvani* theorists, for example, minimize the formal element in poetry.

19.38 *śabda*: Bhartṛhari, *Vākyapadīya* 1.1: "*śabdatattvam . . . vivartate 'tha bhāvena*"

20.1 *śāstra*: The disciplines which take truth (not revelation or delectation) as their aim.

20.1 *ākhyāna*: 'Story', presumably referring to the prose literature. Cf. Dan. 1.28, VSD 6.500.

20.12 *abhipretam*: Kun. text on 1.7. (p. 25/9); "what is meant is a '*sāhitya*' which is different" (scil. from the *sāhitya* of ordinary speech).

20.12 Samudrabandha: A commentator on Ruyyaka who flourished *ca.* A.D. 1300.

20.14 *kāvyam*: Samudrabandha: *Alaṃkārasarvasvavṛtti* p. 4/12 "kāvya is a distinguished [combination of] word and sense."

20.19 *dharma*: 'Property'.

20.20 *lakṣaṇa*: 'Characteristic'; Bharata enumerated thirty-six but distinguished only four *alaṃkāras*. Discussion *infra* page 22 ff.

20.20 *guṇa*: The very early writers Bharata and Bhāmaha are probably meant.

20.22 *kavivyāpāra*: lit. 'poet's *function*'; Bharata relates the *lakṣaṇas* to *kavivyāpāra*. Some sort of poetic intuition is admitted by all writers, but not specifically in this form. (Cf. Vām. 1.3.16; K 1.18.)

20.24 *vyañjanā*: Probably meant are the *Agnipurāna* (342.27), Kuntaka (1.10), Bhoja, and the *Dhvani-kāra*. The terms mean 'strikingness of expression', 'expressiveness', 'enjoyment', 'suggestion'. See Chapter I.

20.32 poetry: see *supra* page 19.

20.39 Rājaśekhara: *Fl. ca.* A.D. 900; poet (both Sanskrit and Prakrit—the *Karpūramanjarī*) who also wrote the curious *Kāvyamīmāṃsā*, which is more a work on the education of the poet than on poetics, and includes a defense of plagiarism.

21.1 poetics: RKM. p. 5/24, p. 4/14; the old myth of the self-division of the primeval man is here given a new application to account for the genera of poetry.

21.9 *śayyā*: Lit. 'bed'.

21.10 refers: *Kādambarī* 1.8: "*sphurattatkalālāpavilāsako-*

> *malā karoti rāgaṃ hṛdi kautukādhikam / rasena śayyāṃ svayam abhyupagatā kathā janasyābhinavā vadhūr iva".*

21.11 *mudrā:* Lit. 'seal'; AP 341.26.

21.14 bed: Apparently K.P. Trivedi, editor of the *Pratāparudrayaśobhūṣana,* his notes, p. 16.

21.15 *maitrī:* From *mitra* 'friend'; VPR 35 (p. 67): "*yā padānaṃ parānyonyamaitrī śayyeti kathyate*".

21.17 metaphor: See note 18.29.

21.20 excellence: VPR 35.

21.23 Vāmana: 1.2.21 *vṛtti.*

21.27 *śabdapāka:* Vām. 1.3.15 *vṛtti;* see *infra* page 42.

21.29 *vaidarbhī rīti:* see note 7.34; the *rītis,* or styles, were at least in origin geographically based.

21.31 real: Vām. 1.2.21 *vṛtti* (stanza 3).

21.35 term: Maṅgala may be meant; a late-ninth-century writer of the *rīti* school whose work is now lost. Cited by RKM p. 20/4–6: "*supāṃ tiñām ca priyā vyutpattiḥ pākaḥ*" Cf. SKD HSP vol. ii 240. Cf. also VEĀ p. 22/3.

21.37 synonym: Vām. 1.3.15 *vṛtti* (stanza 2); also cited by RKM p. 20/10–13.

22.1 sense: VEĀ p. 22/1–4.

22.5 sentiments: VPR 35 (p. 67/9 ff.); Avantisundarī (wife of Rājeśekhara) cited in RKM p. 20/14–20.

22.10 advanced: Chapter III p. 41 ff.

22.10 *śayyā:* For example, VPR (p. 67) (the only writer to treat both) defines *śayyā* as 'friendship of words' and *pāka* (in the following stanza) as 'depth of sense'.

22.12 *lakṣaṇa:* See note 20.20a; Bharata enumerated thirty-six "characteristics" of poetry (NS 16.1 ff.), such as "conciseness" or saying many things in few words (*akṣarasaṃhati*), 'elevated tone' (*śobhā*), 'grandeur' (*abhimāna*), and so forth. The list includes several items which later were accepted as alaṃkāras (*atiśaya,* 'hyperbole'; *hetu* 'etiologia'; *dṛṣṭānta* 'illustration'), but for the most part the concepts involved are aspects of the story or qualities of the dramatis personae. The list played no role in the subsequent history of poetic speculation. Bharata says that the *lakṣaṇas* are to be considered elements of the emotional structure of the drama (*bhāvārthagatāni*) and are to be used as the principal *rasa* dictates. (*samyakprayojyāni yathārasaṃ tu*) (NS 16.4).

22.17 concept: *Some Concepts of the Alankara Sastra,* Adyar (Madras) 1942 pp. 1–47.

22.17   *lakṣaṇapaddhati:* Lit. 'path', here 'school'.
22.19   dramaturgy: Jayadeva, *Candrāloka* and VSD list
        them.
22.22   *lakṣaṇa:* Abh. on NŚ p. 295–8 (vol. 2).
22.23   *bhūṣaṇa:* That is, 'ornament'.
22.24   *sāmudrikalakṣaṇa:* The poses and gestures of the
        dance, each of which has a particular significance.
22.27   *kāvyaśobhākaradharma:* Daṇ. 2.1 cited by Abh. on
        NŚ (vol. 2) p. 295/10.
22.28   *apṛthaksiddha:* Abh. p. 295/15 (vol. 2); emended
        by De, following Rāghavan, to read "*śarīraniṣṭham
        eva yad apṛthaksiddham tal lakṣaṇam*".
22.30   beauty: Abh. p. 295/15 (vol. 2).
22.33   *nāṭakadharma:* 'A property of the drama'; that is,
        considering its place in dramaturgy separate from
        its place in *alaṃkāraśāstra.*
22.33   *saṃdhyaṅgas:* The events of the drama considered
        as bearing on the development of the action. Sixty-
        four are enumerated NŚ ch. 19).
22.34   *daśarūpaka:* by Dhanañjaya (late-tenth-century au-
        thor of the *Daśarūpaka,* a treatise on dramaturgy
        which, though based on, considerably shortens
        Bharata's *Nāṭyaśāstra.* He does not treat the
        alaṃkāras but examines *rasa* at length.)
22.36   *bhāva:* 'Emotion'. Cf. notes 10.33 and 11.15.
22.36   significant: DDR 4.84.
 23.5   Rudraṭa: See notes 2.35 and 2.34.
 23.7   *ālaṃkārika:* Adjectival form.
23.24   embellishment: Cf. Dhv. 1.14.
23.30   Daṇḍin and Vāmana: The two canonical writers of
        the *rīti* school; see note 5.4. Together with Bhā-
        maha (probably earlier) and Udbhaṭa (later)
        they constitute the oldest layer of strictly literary
        speculation.
23.33   *alaṃkāra:* Bhām. 2.4.
23.35   figures: Bhām. 1.36. The term used is *vakrābhi-
        dheyaśabdoktiḥ* 'language involving clever words
        and meanings' or Bhām. 1.30 *vakrasvabhāvokti*
        (*dvandva*) 'clever and natural description'.
 24.6   itself: Cf. Bhām. 1.30.
 24.9   figure *atiśayokti:* Bhām. 2.85: "*saiṣā sarvaiva vakroktir
        anayārtho vibhāvyate / yatno'syāṃ kavinā kāryaḥ
        ko'laṃkāro'nayā vinā*". This is the only mention of
        the term *vakrotki* as such; note singular, referring
        to the previously defined figure (*atiśayokti*).
24.10   *vacaḥ:* 'Speech whose scope exceeds common usage'.
24.11   of *atiśayokti:* Bhām. 2.81.

24.16 life: Ā on Dhv. p. 208/1–5; Abh. on Dhv. p. 208/22
       (these passages refer to Bhām. 2.85 and 1.36, not
       to 2.81); Kuntaka 1.7 and text (De refers to such
       passages as *"tena yat keṣāñcin mataṃ kavikauśa-
       lakalpitakamanīyātiśayaḥ śabda eva kevalam kāv-
       yam. . . . api nirastaṃ bhavati";* the qualification
       in Bhām. 2.81 is not cited as such).
24.23 itself: Abh. on Dhv. p. 280/22–24.
24.26 *alaṃkāras:* Daṇ. 2.363.
24.31 *artha:* Daṇ. 2.1.
24.33 *vañmaya:* Lit. 'verbal stuff'.
24.36 description: Daṇ. 2.363.
24.38 Kuntaka: Kun. 1.11.
 25.1 *pracaksate:* Bhām. 2.93; "Some consider that (*sva-
       bhāvokti* is an *alaṃkāra*)". Cf. Bhām. 1.30.
25.11 *mārga:* Lit. 'road', same as *rīti* (the word is used by
       Vāmana); see notes 5.4, 5.15.
25.12 *Gauḍa:* Dan. 1.40. See note 7.34.
25:13 essence: Daṇ. 1.41–2; on the *guṇas* (properties, vir-
       tues), see note 5.15.
25.17 other: Daṇ. 2.3.
25.19 opinion: NŚ 16.5.
25.24 *mārgas:* Daṇ. 2.3.
25.38 *alaṃkāra:* Vām. 1.1.1.
 26.3 *alaṃkāraḥ:* Vām. 1.1.2.
 26.7 embellishment: Vām. *vṛtti* on 1.1.2.
26.12 *rīti:* Vām. 1.2.8.
26.14 poetry: Vām. 1.2.6.
26.16 *dharmāḥ:* Vām. 3.1.1.
26.17 figures: *supra* page 24.
26.20 *tadatiśayahetavaḥ:* Vām. 3.1.2.
26.21 *nitya:* 'Essential' (lit. 'eternal'); Vām. 3.1.3.
26.25 body: For those not versed in Sanskrit this sentence
       may occasion a few problems, and therefore I
       append a translation: "The stylistic refinements of
       composition, therefore, being the *sine qua non* of
       poetic expression, are described as essential, im-
       plying that the figures of speech are not essential;
       those refinements are properties of the various
       styles, and style is the soul of poetry, while the
       figures are apparently the properties of word and
       sense, which constitutes its body".
26.30 *vartate:* Vām. *vṛtti* on 1.1.1.
26.36 *viśeṣa:* We may recall to the reader that this word
       means 'difference' or 'peculiarity".
26.38 *viśiṣṭapadaracanā:* Vām. 1.2.7.
 27.2 *rīti:* Vām 1.2.7, 11–15.

27.3 Bharata: NŚ 6.25–6; by '*pravṛtti*' Bharata apparently means local variations in dramatic convention and style (Abh. on NŚ p. 269).

27.4 *Pāncālī:* See page 7 ff.

27.31 theorists: Chapter 4.

27.33 Kuntaka: Chapter 3.

28.7 Rudraṭa: See note 5.4.

28.17 phrasing: In the widest sense, including simile, metaphor, hyperbole, etc.

28.29 grammarians: Note 1.16.

28.31 *ālaṃkārika:* Derivative agent noun: 'one who concerns himself with figures of speech'.

28.33 Bharata: Note 4.31.

28.34 Appaya Dīkṣita: late 16th century; his work, the *Kuvalayānanda,* closely follows that of Jayadeva (note 4.31), but adds fifteen figures to his predecessors' total. A useful manual and one still in vogue today.

29.8 *guṇas: supra* page 26 *passim.*

29.11 sense: *supra* page 18.

29.13 arrangement: the word 'arrangement' is qualified by three adjectives: *vyavacchinna, viśiṣṭa,* and '*particular*', all meaning about the same thing. Cf. note 26.36.

29.18 sense: The '*guṇas.*'

29.34 produced: Cf. Mam. 1.3 (p. 9/2).

30.4 intuition: Cf. Daṇ. 2.364–6.

30.17 *doṣas:* See page 6.

30.35 others: Vāmana.

31.8 *alaṃkārya:* 'A possessor of the quality' and 'a thing to be ornamented'.

31.12 poetry: Ā on Dhv. 3.52 p. 231/10–13.

31.21 ornaments: Cf. Dhv. 3.32–3.

31.27 types: Kun. 1.24 text (p. 22/8 ff.).

31.33 poets: Kun. 1.24 text (p. 101/4 ff.); 1.57 (p. 163/8–11).

32.2 characteristics: Daṇ. 1.101; 2.1.

32.5 *Gauḍī:* Daṇ. 1.40.

32.7 qualities: Vām. 1.2.13, 14.

32.8 forth: See page 7 and notes.

32.18 consistent: Mam. ch. 8. Mammaṭa is the latter-eleventh-century author of the *Kāvyaprakāśa,* the standard work, in India at any rate, on the subject of poetics. He follows Ānandavardhana and Abhinavagupta in the main (notes 8.13 and 8.26), and it was his work which was largely responsible for the triumph of the *dhvani* theory. The *Prakāśa* however has in itself very little merit, being an encyclopaedic compilation of previously discussed topics, put together with very little regard for either their nature or consistency. The work has (probably) more commentaries than any other Indian book (SKD HSP vol. i, 156 ff.) and has served as model for other writers of encyclopaedic bent (notably VSD, note 14.35, HKA note 55.18, and VEĀ, note 59.27.

32.27 practice: Kun. 1.24 text (p. 99/2-p. 102/3).
32.35 multiplication: Kun. 1.24 *text* (p. 102/7 ff.).

NOTES TO CHAPTER 3. THE POETIC IMAGINATION

33.3 described: Chapter 1.
34.10 Bhaṭṭa Nāyaka: Early tenth century, author of the Hṛdayadarpaṇa.
34.14 partially: The first two chapters complete, parts of the third, and fragments of the last. *Vakroktijīvita*, ed. S.K. De (2nd ed.) Calcutta 1928.
34.19 poet: Cf. Chapter 2.
34.20 *vakrokti*: Lit. '*expression courbée*,' 'indirect speech'.
34.21 Bhāmaha: 2.85; here a synonym for 'hyperbole' (*atiśayokti*) and apparently concomitant with all other *alaṃkāras* (*ko'laṃkāro'nayā vinā*).
34.27 speech: Kun. 1.10.
34.28 name: Kun. 1.20, 1.23; that is, the phrase *vakrokti* as a collective name for the *alaṃkāras*.
34.31 sense: Kun. 1.7; 1.10.
34.32 exclusively: For example, certain stories or situations are in themselves "poetic." Kun. text on 1.21 (p. 90/7 ff.) as when Sītā remaining alone sends Lakṣmaṇa to investigate a pitiable wailing knowing full well that the forest contains a dangerous enemy.
34.35 nonessential: Kun. text on 1.20 (p. 89/7 ff.), on 1.7 (p. 28/11 ff.; cites Bhāmaha) (p. 33/1 ff.). See also note 35.13.
34.36 poet: Skt. "*kavivyāpāra*" (Kun. 1.18). See notes 20.22 and 20.24.
34.37 letters: *Varṇavinyāsavakratvam* Kun. 1.19.
34.37 base: *Padapūrvārdhavakratā* Kun. 1.19.
34.38 termination: *pratyayāśrayaḥ* (*prakāraḥ*) Kun. 1.19.
34.38 sentence: *Vākya* Kun. 1.20.
34.38 topic: *Prakaraṇa* Kun. 1.21.
35.1 whole: *Prabandha* Kun. 1.21.

35.11 *śāstra:* Kun. 1.5 and text. See also note 20.1. Cf. Abh. on Dhv. p. 70/9–20.

35.13 speech: Kun 1.8; curiously enough, the commentary includes in "common speech" the function of suggestion! (*vyañjakavyaṅgya*).

35.17 *bhaṅgībhaṇiti:* Kun. 1.10; lit. 'circumlocutory speech'; *bhaṅgī* and *vakra* both mean 'curve' or 'curved'.

35.20 *vicchitti:* Kun. 1.18 *vicchittisobhinaḥ* of the *kārikā* is glossed as *vaicitryabhaṅgībhrājiṣnavaḥ.*

35.21 *vidagdha:* lit. 'burned up', 'consumed' from root *vi-dah-;* 'tempered', 'seasoned', 'clever'. Compare our use of the word 'sharp'. Kun. 1.10; a synonym for *sahṛdaya.*

35.23 scholar: Cf. Kun. 1.5. He uses the word *tadvit* ('who knows that') as a synonym for *vidagdha.* Cf. Ā on Dhv. p. 239/18 where the terms seem to be complimentary; and SKD HSP vol. ii, p. 186, note 12.

35.24 *pratibhā:* Kun. 1.34; Comm. on 1.7 (p. 32/11).

35.25 *kauśala:* Kun. Comm. on 1.10 (p. 51/8–9).

35.26 *kavivyāpāra:* Kun. 1.18; glossed as *kāvyakriyālakṣaṇah.*

35.34 imagination: Kun. Comm. on 1.7 (p. 18/8 ff.); an example is given which despite many formal devices does not please.

35.36 other: Kun. Comm. on 1.2 (p. 8/1–6).

36.1 *vaicitrya:* Kun. Comm. on 1.10 (p. 51/11).

36.2 *kavipratibhānirvartitatva:* Source unknown.

36.5 poet: Kun. Comm. on 1.7 (p. 32/10–11).

36.10 itself: Kun. 1.13.

36.31 expression: Kun. Comm. on 1.3 (p. 8/2).

37.13 Ruyyaka: mid-twelfth century, author of the *Alaṃkārasarvasva,* a late work on the *alaṃkāras* important for its precision and thoroughness.

37.15 figure: Ruy. AS p. 184/2.

37.17 *anumāna:* That is, 'inference'. Ruy. AS p. 184/3.

37.19 *saṃdeha:* That is, 'doubt'; Ruy. AS p. 53/8.

37.30 Ānandavardhana: See note 15.13. Cf. Abh. on Dhv. p. 70/4–6.

37.30 Kuntaka: Kun. 1.18.

37.33 production: JRGĀ p. 6/2 ff.

37.37 *sāmājika:* from *samāj* 'assembly', 'one of the assembly'.

38.30 description: Kun. 1.11; see *supra* page 24 ff.

38.36 *kaviprauḍhokti:* 'Over-ornateness'. Cf. Dhv. 2.27.

39.3 Rājaśekhara: See note 20.39.

39.12 death: RKM p. 21/4.

39.14 *kāvya:* See pages 20 and 35.

39.17   *kāvyakavi:* RKM p. 17/6 ff.

39.27   *pratibhā:* See note 35.24.

39.28   illuminates: RKM p. 11/24; "*yā . . . pratibhāsayati sā pratibhā*".

39.29   poet: RKM p. 11/25, p. 12/1.

39.30   things: RKM p. 12/2–3.

39.33   *bhāvayitrī:* agent nouns from the causative aspect of *kṛ-* 'to do' and *bhū-* 'to be'. Cf. page 50.

39.34   production: RKM p. 12/20, p. 13/21.

40.1   Mahimabhaṭṭa: Latter-eleventh-century author of the *Vyaktiviveka,* who attempts to account for poetic allusion (*dhvani*) in terms of inference (*anumiti*). He is one of the few writers of the late period to question the function of suggestion.

40.5   form: *Vyaktiviveka* p. 32/19–25; "*anumeyārthasaṃsparśamātraṃ cānvayavyatirekābhyāṃ kāvyasya cārutvahetur niscitam*".

40.13   Kṣemendra: Mid-eleventh-century writer of prolific capacity and universal interests. Perhaps his best-known work is the *Bṛhatkathāmañjarī,* a Sanskrit version of the "Great Story", but he wrote also on philosophical and religious subjects (see list SKD HSP vol. i, p. 132–3). His two works on poetics are the *Aucityavicāracarcā* and the *Kavikaṇṭhābharaṇa,* which fall into the category of *kaviśikṣā,* or the education of the poet. See note 20.39.

40.16   Ānandavardhana: *Supra* page 15 ff.

40.18   itself: AVC 3–5.

40.21   poetry: AVC 5.

40.29   forth: AVC 8–10 and severally throughout the rest of the work.

40.31   number: *Ibid.*

41.1   Ānandavardhana: Ā on Dhv. p. 148/7–9 (with Abh. on Dhv. p. 148/19/20).

41.4   poem: AVC text on verse 13 (p. 120/22 ff.).

41.5   work: *Kumārasaṃbhava* 3.72.

41.9   god: 'Bhava' means approximately 'being' and 'rudra' 'roarer'; both are epithets of Śiva.

41.14   *pāka:* Lit. 'bed' and 'ripeness'; chapter 2, p. 21 ff.

41.24   *Śayyā:* See page 21 and note.

41.25   connotation: See page 21 and note 21.10.

41.27   bed: See page 21.

41.31   synonyms: See *supra* page 21; VPR, p. 67/8.

41.38   excellence: See page 21.

42.3   Vāmana: See page 21.

42.4   *śabdapāka:* See page 21.

42.6   *rīti:* See pages 21 and 7.

42.8   real: See page 21.
42.10   synonym: See page 21.
42.13   sense: See page 22.
42.17   sentiments: See page 22. *"Arthapāka"* probably coined by De.
42.18   *śabdavyutpatti:* See page 21.
42.19   Rājaśekhara: *Supra* page 39: note 20.39.
42.23   *Ācarya:* 'Teachers', 'sages'.
42.23   Maṅgala: See note 21.35.
42.30   successful: Vām. 1.3.15; See *supra* and page 21.
42.32   synonyms: Vām. *ibid;* the entire quotation is from RKM p. 20/4 ff.
43.5   Avantisundarī: Wife of Rājasekhara and obviously a very talented lady.
43.24   *sahṛdaya:* RKM pp. 20/14 ff.; on the *sahṛdaya* see note 51.25 and page 54 passim.
44.3   *vṛntākapāka:* Vām. 3.2.14 *vṛtti;* he also mentions *cūta* (mango) and *dāḍima* (pomegranate), likening the best poetry to the taste of the mango, poetry employing verbal device to the eggplant, and poetry lacking all quality to the pomegranate.
44.8   *nimba:* RKM p. 20/23 ff.; AP 346.22–3; VPR p. 67/11; in Rājaśekhara nine types are given, according as the "taste" in the drama develops from bitter to sweet, from bitter to neutral, from sweet to bitter, etc.
44.13   Bhoja: Chapter 4 p. 59; see notes 59.22, 59.27.
44.15   *dhvani* theorists: those who emphasize the allusive or suggestive element in poetry: see note 8.13 and Chapters 1 and 4 *passim.* Rudrabhaṭṭa and Bhoja are not meant.
44.27   constituents: 53.15.
44.36   essential: Cf. BSKĀ 5.1–2.
45.5   *rasa:* BSKĀ 5.1: *Rasa* is said to be a synonym of *śṛṅgāra.*
45.8   *Śṛṅgāratilaka:* Note 59.22.
45.18   Rūpa Gosvāmin: Early-sixteenth-century Vaiṣṇava writer.
45.25   internal: Daṇḍin, for example, divides poetry (*kāvya*) into prose (*gadya*), verse (*padya*) and mixed (*miśra*); Dan. 1.11.
46.32   Mammaṭa: See note 32.18.
46.32   Viśvanātha: Note 14.35.
46.36   Jagannātha: Note 15.1.
47.5   sense: ĪRGĀ p. 6/3: *"ramaṇiyārthapratipādakaḥ sabdaḥ kavyam";* see 58.39 and Chapter 4 *passim.*

47.7 experience: JRGĀ p. 6/3–4: "*ramaṇiyatā ca lokotta-rāhlādajanakajñānagocaratā*".
47.9 itself: JRGĀ p. 6/6–7.
47.12 objects: JRGĀ p. 6/7–9.
47.17 stimulus: JRGĀ p. 12/4 ff.

NOTES TO CHAPTER 4. AESTHETIC ENJOYMENT

48.1 *rasa:* See Chapter I.
48.4 Bharata: NŚ Ch. 6.
48.5 Viśvanātha: VSD 1.3.
48.11 words: Dhv. 1.3.
48.12 listener: Dhv. 1.4.
48.15 *vyañjanā:* See note 8.29 and in general Chapter 1.
48.16 poetry: Dhv. 1.1.
48.19 expressed: See note 13.39 and text.
48.27 recognized: In treating all figures except *yamaka* (Vām. 4.1.1 ff.) as extensions of simile (Vām. 4.3.1 ff.).
48.30 such: Dhv. 1.14–15, 19.
48.31 unexpressed: Dhv. 1.16, 18.
49.12 directly: Dhv. Comm. on 1.4 (p. 99/1); Dhv. 2.3, 24–26. An example of a suggested *alaṃkāra* would be, "The summer yawns and wilts the lazy flowers with his tepid breath"; where a simile is understood: the summer is like a person with bad breath. Of course, these implicit similes are always understood as such by the *alaṃkāra* writers. This one would be called an *utprekṣā. Rasa* differs from *alaṃkāra* and *vastu* in that it is incapable of being so transformed into a literal statement. The utterance "love" does not express the *rasa* 'love.'
49.13 feelings: See note 11.15 and *passim* in Chapter 1.
49.14 *dhvani:* Ā on Dhv. p. 163/7–9.
49.23 *vibhāvas:* See note 11.30.
49.28 *alaukika:* See note 12.13.
49.37 dictum: "*na hi rasād ṛte kaścid arthaḥ pravartate/ tatra vibhāvānubhāvavyabhicārisaṃyogād rasani-ṣpattiḥ*" (NŚ, *sūtra* following 6.31). This, the so-called *rasasūtra,* is the occasion for Abhinava-gupta's brilliant discursus on the nature of *rasa* (NŚ p. 272).
50.2 *abhivyakti:* lit. 'manifestation', another word for 'suggestion'. Abh. by KPK p. 96/9–10. Abh. on Dhv. p. 70/22, p. 71/1.
50.2 Bhaṭṭa Nāyaka's theory: In the lost *Hṛdayadarpaṇa;*

an author of the beginning of the tenth century, who attempted to refute the *dhvani*. Abhinavagupta nevertheless respects his views and takes much trouble accounting for his criticisms, notably in his Comm. on NŚ p. 276/19 ff.

50.5   *bhogīkaraṇa:* 'the power of enlivening' (from *bhāva* 'emotion') and 'making enjoyable' (*bhoga* 'enjoyment'). A succinct restatement of Bhaṭṭa Nāyaka's view is given in NŚ p. 277/1 ff.

50.6   *rasavyañjanā:* 'The suggestion of *rasa*'; Abh. on Dhv. 70/6–7; Abh. on NŚ p. 277/18 ff.

50.6   *āsvāda:* See Chapter I; one of the higher intellectual states whose essence is to be *rasa*. A confusing multiplicity of such words occur: *āsvāda, carvaṇā, rasanā, camatkāra*, etc. *Āsvāda* does not imply that there is a state beyond *rasa* whose property is to comprehend the *rasa* (VSD 3.60 text). Abh. on Dhv. p. 70/15.

50.7   *bhāvāḥ:* "The *bhāvas* are so called because they enliven the sense of the poem", NŚ text preceding 7.1 (p. 342); Bharata is speaking from the point of view of the dramatist.

50.9   *dhātuḥ:* "The root *bhū-* ('to be') is to be taken in a causative sense"; Bharata, NŚ text preceding 7.1 (p. 344).

50.10   *vyāptyartham:* Bhar. NŚ. (p. 345).

50.10   poetry: Abh. on Dhv. p. 70/8–10.

50.12   *sthāyin:* The *bhāva* itself, distinguished from its accessories (See note 11.30) is called *sthāyibhāva* 'fixed emotion', that is, necessarily implying a certain rasa, as love must imply the erotic *rasa* only. The *vyabhicāribhāvas* are not so determined.

50.14   poetry: Abh. on Dhv. p. 68/19–21.

50.15   *āsvādayati:* 'he enjoys (it) in a completely general way' (source unknown).

50.17   *niṣpādaka:* 'producer' from *niṣpatti* 'origin' (in Bharata's *sūtra*).

50.17   *rasa:* Abh. on Dhv. p. 69/13–15.

50.18   *bhāvakatva:* -*tva* is a general nominalizing suffix; English "-ness."

50.18   Abhinava: Shorter form of Abhinavagupta.

50.19   *guṇa:* See note 5.15.

50.21   sense: Abh. on Dhv. p. 70/12–13.

50.26   *bhoga:* Abh. on NŚ p. 277/7; Abh. on Dhv. p. 70/5–8.

50.31   employed: Abh. on NŚ p. 285/2–3; Abh. on Dhv. p. 69/17–20 [this list omits *upamiti* ('comparison') and includes "*yogapratyakṣajā pratītiḥ*" ('yogic perception')]; the term *pratibhāna* means 'imagination' (cf. *pratibhā*, note 35.24), the other terms are the usual four "*pramāṇas*" or modes of cognition of the Logics (See note 19.27): perception, inference, comparison, and revelation.

50.33   *rati,* etc.: Abh. on Dhv. p. 70/14–17.

51.1   functions: Abh. on Dhv. p. 70/18–19, on NŚ p. 277/11 ff.

51.5   functions: Abh. on Dhv. p. 70/14, 19.

51.13   *śabdārthasāhitya:* Chapter II; note 18.22.

51.25   *sāmājika:* See note 37.37.

51.25   *sahṛdaya:* Lit. 'sharing the heart'; one who through education and sensibility is a proper connoisseur of the *rasa;* the critical audience. Abh. on NŚ p. 281/12, p. 287/7 ff.

51.36   fact: cf. Abh. on Dhv. p. 29/17.

52.2   *carvaṇā: Supra, passim.*

52.7   *laukika:* 'exoteric'.

52.9   causes: Abh. on NŚ p. 284/6–10, p. 285/1–2; Also see note 12.13.

52.12   essential: Abh. on NŚ p. 284/1–3, p. 282/9; 'pity', 'disgust', and 'horror' are translations of the three Sanskrit terms.

52.17   pain: VSD 3.35 ff.

52.20   Visvanātha: See note 14.35.

52.26   dalliance: VSD 3.57 and text.

52.29   sentiment: VSD 3.38.

52.29   Jagannātha: See note 15.1.

52.34   pain: JRGĀ p. 45/7–10.

52.38   means: JRGĀ p. 45/13, p. 46/1.

53.6   *rasa:* See Chapter 1 and notes pp. 11–14 *passim.*

53.7   *vibhāvas,* etc.: *Vibhāva* is the *name* applied to those ordinary causes (gardens, the beloved, etc.) when they are given extraordinary representation, as in a poem. Abh. on NŚ p. 284/7–9.

53.15   constituents: E.g., VSD, text following 3.46.

53.22   impressions: Abh. on NŚ p. 285/23, p. 284/6; see note 12.8.

53.27   connexions: Abh. on Dhv. p. 70/4–5, on NŚ p.285/6–7. Cf. DDR 4.41.

53.33   drama: *Supra* note 50.21.

53.39   limitations: Abh. on NŚ p. 285/6–8, p. 279/1–16.

54.1   generalized: This sequence of generalizations is reasoned out in Abh. by KPK p. 98/5 ff.

54.5   sensibility: Abh. on NŚ p. 279/13–14; VSD 3.60 and text. See also note 51.25.

54.11 *sādhāraṇīkaraṇa:* 'universality' or 'universalizing'; see note 12.29.
54.14 poetry: Abh. by KPK p. 97/4–6.
54.16 *naisargikī:* From *Svabhāva* 'nature' and *nisarga* 'origin'; Abh. by KPK p. 97/7; Daṇ. 1.103 (*pratibhā*).
54.16 experience: SD 3.39 text.
54.18 *mīmāṃsakas:* See note 13.39.
54.20 *yogāḥ:* "Only connoisseurs of the *rasa* are capable of realising the *rasa*." (source unknown)
54.21 actor: VSD 3.49.
54.22 Dhanañjaya: See note 22.34.
54.23 enjoyment: DDR 4.36 text.
54.25 *adhikārin:* 'Official' (one who holds an office), hence 'authority'.
54.25 *pramātṛ:* 'giver of criteria'; cf. *pramāṇa* (note 19.27); VSD 3.60 text/8; JRGĀ p. 37/10.
54.28 *hṛdayaḥ:* "The authority is one whose mind is capable of flawless imagination" (i.e., permitting total absorption in the poetic creation). Abh. on NŚ p. 279/1.
54.31 *sahṛdayaḥ:* "The connoisseur participates in the consensus of minds and is one who has perceived the natural appropriateness of what is represented. His mind has become lucidly receptive like a mirror, through effort and constant practice of poetry". Abh. on Dhv. p. 11/23–4.
55.18 grammarians: Mam. 5.69 text; HKA p. 49; VEĀ ch. 1 p. 23–53, etc.; also Abh. on NŚ p. 280/3–4, Abh. on Dhv. p. 17–19.
55.20 *vyañjanāvṛtti:* The 'mode of existence' of suggestion; *vartate* 'it exists in a certain fashion'.
55.21 *abhivyakti:* Note 50.2.
55.22 *carvanā:* Abh. by KPK p. 99/56; also see note 50.7.
55.22 *vītavighnapratīti:* Abh. on NŚ p. 280/8; he says "*sarvathā rasanātmakavītavighnapratītigrāyho bhāva eva rasaḥ.*" *Abhivyakti* is inferred as the subject.
55.27 *ratyādīn:* JRGĀ p. 37/14 ff; "This comprehension (*vyakti*) is unhindered intelligence; as in the opinion of the 'arrow' school a shielded light illuminates adjacent objects when the shield is removed, and likewise reveals itself, just so does the intelligence (*ātmacaitanyam*) illuminate the circumstance of the drama, the enacted emotions, etc. (and reveal itself)". Cf. Dhv. 1.9. The "arrow" school refers to

a theory of denotation by which all the meanings, literal, conventional, and allusive, at any time attachable to a word, should be considered no more than the literal meaning extending itself farther and farther (in the manner of an arrow) to the goal set by the speaker's intention. This theory was often resorted to by those denying the function of suggestion (*vyanjanā* or *abhivyakti*). Cf. Mam. text on 5.69 (p. 213/4 ff.).

55.28 *Prabhā:* That is, Vaidyanātha, who composed the *Kāvyaprakāśapradīpaprabhā* a commentary on the *Kāvyaprakāśapradīpa* written by Govinda Ṭhakkura (late fifteenth century), which is itself a commentary on Mammaṭa's *Kāvyaprakāśa.* Should not be confused with Vidyānātha, author of the *Pratāparudrayaśobhūṣaṇa.*

55.30 *cit:* Vaidyanātha p. 80/23–4 (see previous note); "this poetic delectation (*carvaṇā*) is a manifestation of (pure) thought in erotically defined circumstances, accompanied by appropriate *vibhāvas, anubhāvas,* etc. and it is this thought freed from obstacles." These "obstacles" are generally in the form of states of mind which prevent the full participation of the onlooker in the unfolding of the drama. See next.

55.33 *vighnāpasāraka:* Abh. on NŚ p. 280/9; 'removers of obstacles'. Abhinava here describes the various obstacles to sympathetic cognition: lack of imagination; predisposition to regard what is going on on the stage as mere historical fact; lack of interest; lack of experience; unfamiliarity with the language used; portrayal of some trifling matter which does not concern the universality of human experience; confusion as to the emotion being portrayed.

55.36 repose: all these from one line of Abh. on NŚ p. 280/10.

55.38 *carvyamānaikaprāṇaḥ:* Cf. note 13.8; "whose life consists entirely of being enjoyed" VEA p. 88/1–2; (as "*carvyamānataikaprāṇatayā*") Abh. cited by KPK p. 99/6; (as "*carvyamānataikasāraḥ*") (same meaning); Abh. on NŚ p. 284/11.

55.38 *alaukika:* See note 12.13.

56.4 *vigalitavedyāntara:* VEA p. 87/5 (as "*-āntaratvena*")

56.6 *vedyāntarasparśaśūnya:* VSD 3.34 (as *vedyāntarasamparkaśūnya* Abh. by KPK p. 100/8).

56.7   Brahma: See note 13.12.

56.10 itself: See notes 13.8, 13.28, and 55.27.

56.13 *gocarīkṛtah:* "Realized by the critic (*pramātṛ:* see note 54.25) who participates in the consensus of all connoisseurs" Mam. p. 98/3–p. 99/1 (this phrase is part of a much longer definition of *rasa*).

56.15 life breath: See note 55.27.

56.15 *camatkāra:* Lit. 'astounding', 'causing astonishment' (see note 50.6) but usually, 'striking' 'charming'.

56.16 Viśvanātha: See note 14.35.

56.19 *paryāyah:* VSD text following 3.34 (p. 51/6–7); *vismaya,* here translated 'wonder', is the *sthāyibhāva* (note 50.12) corresponding to the *rasa adbhuta* 'marvellous'.

56.20 *rasah:* "wherever this strikingness (*camatkāra*) is found as an essential element, there you have *adbhutarasa*" (see previous note); this is part of a *śloka* quoted by VSD (p. 51/10) and attributed to one Dharmadatta, who is citing Viśvanātha's great-grandfather, Nārāyaṇa, as being of the opinion that the *adbhutarasa* (the 'marvellous') is an essential element in all the other *rasas*.

56.22 *vicchitti:* See 35.20.

56.25 *kavipratibhā:* See page 35 ff.

56.26 figures: JRGĀ p. 12/4 ff; p. 13/1–3; p. 248/3–5; cf. Dhv. 2.6; and cf. Abh. on Dhv. p. 13/18 ff.

56.28 *anubhavasākṣika:* JRGĀ p. 6/5–6.

56.29 *alaukikāhlāda:* JRGĀ p. 6/4, 5 ("*lokottarāhlāda*").

57.3   shape: VSD 3.34; compare the analogy of the light: note 55.27.

57.7   *rasasaṃtatim:* "Those having merit experience, like ascetics, the plentitude of rasa" lit.: "to the meritorious as to yogis is vouschafed the continuity of delectation" VSD p. 52/2–3 (cited immediately after the quote in 56.19 and attributed to someone else).

57.17 Mahimabhaṭṭa: See note 40.1.

57.22 poetry: MVV p. 22/10; Mahimabhaṭṭa even suggests that the Dhvanikāra rephrase his definition of *dhvani* (1.1) so as not to imply that some people deny the importance of *rasa;* MVV p. 110/5–8.

57.23 school: See note 8.26 and 5.4.

57.33 *alaṃkāradhvani:* See page 49.

57.39 *asti:* Abh. on Dhv. (2.3) p. 65/6.

58.1   *kāvyam:* Abh. on Dhv. (2.3) p. 65/6–7.

58.6   poetry: Abh. on Dhv. (1.4) p. 15/17–18; p. 27/3.
58.10 poetry: VSD 1.3.
58.18 poets: JRGĀ p. 12/4–7.
58.20 *rasābhāsa:* VSD text on 1.2 (p. 13/14); 3.247.
58.21 *vastudhvani: Attā ettha nimajjai ettha ahaṃ diasaaṃ paloehi / mā pahia rattiandhaa sejjāe mahamṇa majjahisi"* 'my mother-in-law sleeps here and I sleep there; how late the day has become! Now watch out lest you, blinded by the gloom of evening, get into one of our beds!' (spoken by an improperly libidinous young lady [whose husband is travelling] to a male visitor to whom the honors of the guest have been offered.) The situation (*vastu*) suggested here is of course that of an invitation; the visitor, though the grammatical form is that of a warning, is thus caused to remark the disposition of the two beds and is in fact told not to get into the wrong one. The verse is cited by Ānandavardhana as proof that the intention of an utterance is not always the same as its literal import (p. 20/2–3). Repeated by VSD, 1.2 text (p. 13/11).
58.24 poetry: VSD p. 13/13; p. 15/4 ff.; the term *"rasa-sparśa"* from JRGĀ (p. 12/10–11), not Viśvanātha.
58.27 leaps: JRGĀ p. 12/11.
58.30 the *rasa:* JRGĀ p. 12/12–13; see note 11.30.
58.36 about *rasa:* JRGĀ p. 48/4–p. 49/4.
58.39 *śabdaḥ:* 'Words productive of delightful effect' or 'expressing agreeable meanings'; JRGĀ p. 6/3.
59.3   poetry: JRGĀ p. 50/1–3; *ramaṇiyatā* means literally 'the state of being conducive to pleasure'.
59.7   Mammaṭa: See note 32.18.
59.12 writers: Chapter 3 p. 44 ff.
59.22 *Śṛṅgāratilaka:* A work of uncertain date, perhaps at the end of the tenth century (SKD HSP vol. i p. 91); the author was once thought to be the same person as Rudraṭa (note 18.16) but is now considered not to be.
59.24 poetry: RŚT 1.5.
59.27 *Śṛṅgāraprakāśa:* First half of the eleventh century; probably none other than King Bhoja of Dārā, a well-known patron of letters and the arts. The work has the dubious distinction of being the longest ever written on the subject of poetics. It is unpublished, but a résumé by V. Rāghavan is available (*New Ind. Antiquary* v. 1–4). Bhoja is also

the author of the *Sarasvatīkaṇṭhābharaṇa,* which though largely copied from earlier authors, appears to conserve some traces of the independent poetic doctrine of the *Agnipurāṇa.*

59.27 Vidyādhāra: *Ca.* 1300, author of the *Ekāvali,* a treatise based primarily on Mammaṭa (note 32.18) and Ruyyaka (note 37.13) and affirming the primordinance of *dhvani.*

59.28 Kumārasvāmin: Early-fifteenth-century commentator of Vidyānātha's *Pratāparudrayaśobhūṣaṇa.*

59.35 Śāradātanaya: Twelfth or thirteenth century.

59.37 Śiṅgabhūpāla: Early fourteenth century.

59.39 Rasataraṅgiṇī: Latter half of the fifteenth century.

60.8 *nāyikā:* The ideal hero and heroine.

60.33 *Ujjvalanīlamaṇi:* See note 45.18.

60.35 *ujjvala:* Lit. 'incandescence', 'bursting into flame'.

60.35 *madhurarasa:* Lit. 'sweet'; originally one of Daṇḍin's ten *guṇas* (note 5.17)

60.37 *rasa: Ujjvalaveṣātmakaḥ,* 'whose essence is an appearance of burning' (i.e. "inflamed" passions, etc.) NŚ text on 6.45 (p. 300/1).

61.1 *bhaktirasaḥ: Ujjvalanīlamaṇi* 1.3; that is, the state of religious devotion considered as a *rasa.* A turnabout of the theory (cf. page 13 and note 13.12).

61.6 sweetness: Of these the first (*śānta*) is the much-discussed ninth *rasa* of the canonical schools and *mādhurya* ('sweetness', nominalization of *madhura*) is a *guṇa; preyas* is also the name of an *alaṃkāra* (Daṇ. 2.275), and *prīti* is a definand of *rasavadalaṃkāra,* one of the most controversial figures (Daṇ. 2.281; Dhv. 2.5).

61.7 *bhaktirasarāṭ:* "King" of *bhakti rasas* (the five listed). UN 1.2.

61.9 *sthāyibhāva:* See page 50; *rati* ('physical passion') is the fixed emotion corresponding to *śṛṅgārarasa,* or the erotic sentiment.

61.21 hero: UN 1.18–20.

NOTES TO CHAPTER 5. CREATION AND RE-CREATION

62.5 wide: Bhavabhūti, *Mālatīmādhavam* 1.8; *"utpatsyate mama tu ko'pi samānadharmā kālo hy ayaṃ niravadhir vipulā ca pṛthvī".*

62.21 productive: Cf. Abh. on Dhv. p. 29/17–18.

63.13   *sahṛdaya:* Notes 51.25, 54.31; Chapter 4 *passim.*
63.17   creation: Abh. on Dhv. p. 11/24; see note 54.31.
63.24   *rasayitṛ:* Abh. on Dhv. p. 12/5; agent nouns of the
        causative aspects of the roots *budh-* 'know' and
        ras- 'taste'.
63.29   *viśadībhūtamanomukura:* Abh. on Dhv. p. 11/23; see
        note 54.31. "manomukura" Lit. 'mind-mirror'.
64.10   word: From *ras-* 'taste' cf. *rasanā,* the 'tongue'.
64.12   *carvaṇā:* See note 50.6.
65.15   *guṇa-rīti:* 'poetic excellence' and 'style': note 5.4 and
        Chapter II; *vakrokti* is 'indirect speech': note 34.20
        and Chapter II; *pakā:* Note 41.14 and Chapters II
        and III; *dhvani* is 'suggestion': notes 10.33 and
        11.15 and Chapters I and IV; *rasa* is 'aesthetic
        delectation': notes 10.33 and 11.15 and Chapters
        1 and 4.
66.13   conduct: Mam. 1.2 (p. 5).
66.17   life: VSD 1.2.
66.27   mistress: Mam. p. 6/4.
66.30   palatable: Aśvaghoṣa, *Saundarananda* 18.63; Aśva-
        ghoṣa lived in the first century A.D., was a Bud-
        dhist, and is the first known writer of *kāvya*
        (ornate poetry).
68.20   significance: Cf. Vām. 2.1.15; Mam. p. 256/2 ff.
 69.9   *alaukika:* Note 12.13.
69.12   bliss: Mam. 1.1. "*niyatikṛtaniyamarahitāṃ hlādai-
        kamayīm . . . nirmitim*".
69.21   *ānanda:* Supra page 55.
69.25   deliverer: Abh. on NŚ p. 282/3.
72.16   same: Cf. RKM p. 17–19.
72.21   *Raghuvaṃśa:* "No composition of Kālidāsa displays
        more the richness of his poetical genius, the exu-
        berance of his imagination, the warmth and play
        of his fancy, his profound knowledge of the human
        heart, his delicate appreciation of its most refined
        and tender emotions, his familiarity with the work-
        ings and counter-workings of its conflicting feeling,
        —in sort, more entitle him to rank as the Shake-
        speare of India". (M. Monier-Williams). Said in
        reference to the *Śakuntalā* but cited by the ed. of
        the *Raghuvaṃśa!*
72.21   *Naiṣadha:* "Vaste épopée en 22 chants, qui, sous
        pretexte de narrer l'épisode de Nala et Damayantī,
        multiplie les dissertations sur des sujets philo-
        sophiques ou techniques, attestant d'ailleurs une
        maîtrise éclatante en nombre de śāstra; . . . Au

chant XVII, les dieux qui ont pris part au *sva-yaṃvara* décrivent les diverses doctrines dont ils se font les protagonistes, et l'ensemble du poème forme une sorte de cursus religieux et philoso-phique, où ne manquent pas des illusions, relative-ment insolites, aux materialistes, à Dattātreya, aux douze idoles de Viṣṇu, à la déesse bouddhique Tārā, etc" (Louis Renou). The author of the *Naiṣadha* is Śrīharṣa.

72.30   *Kumārasaṃbhava:* Another epic poem of Kalidāsa. "The theme is truly a daring one in aspiring to en-compass the love of the highest deities; . . . The new mythology had life, warmth, and colour, and brought the gods nearer to human life and emo-tion. The magnificent figure of the divine ascetic (Śiva), scorning love but ultimately yielding to its humanising influence, the myth of his temptation leading to the destruction of Kāma as the emblem of human desire, the story of Umā's resolve to win by renunciation what her beauty and love could not achieve by their seduction . . . " (S. K. De).

73.1   *pratibhā:* Notes 35.24; 50.31.

73.7   ridiculous: Vām. 1.3.16.

73.13   poetry: Abh. on Dhv. p. 29/18–19: *"pratibhā apūrva-vastunirmāṇakṣamā prajñā".*

73.15   poet: Bharata is explaining the sense in which he uses the word *bhāva* ('emotion'): *"vāgaṅgamukha-rāgeṇa sattvenābhinayena ca / kaver antargataṃ bhāvaṃ bhāvayan bhāva ucyate"* NŚ 7.2.

73.24   objects: *Supra* pages 24, 38.

73.27   account: Daṇ. 2.8 ff.

73.29   *bhāvika:* Lit. 'expressive', 'real'; a figure defined as *prabandhaviṣayo guṇaḥ* (*text* in accusative) 'a quality of the entire work', and which is perceived in such aspects as the relevance of the various parts of the story to one another, the clarification of difficult contexts by emphasizing a chain of events, the suitability of the story to representa-tion, clarity of language, and so forth. Daṇḍin ex-plains that this "figure" is a function of the poet's intention or desire (*abhiprāya*), and can be seen as a competent rendering of that unifying prin-ciple in the work. Bhām. 3.52; Daṇ. 2.364 ff.

73.30   quality: *Guṇa.*

73.35   imagination: Chapter 3.

73.37   *kavikarman: Supra* page 35.

74.23   expressed: Note 8.26.
74.34   abstraction: In fact, they affirm the contrary: *supra*
pages 53 ff., 12 ff.
75.8   poetry: *Supra* page 66.
75.27   *praitbhā*: Cf. Rud. 1.14, Mam. 1.3, etc. HKA p. 6.
75.37   culture: Rud. 1.16 (he does say, however, that inborn imagination is preferable).
76.5   stones: Rud. 1.18, Mam. p. 8/2 ff., Vām. 1.3.3, RKM
ch. 8.
76.17   practices: HKA p. 9/12 ff.; AKK
76.25   craft: The chief among whom was Arisiṃha, a Jain
writer of the thirteenth century; but Rājaśekhara
and Kṣemendra also treat of the subject. See notes
20.39 and 40.13.
78.13   grammar: See note 1.16.

BIBLIOGRAPHY

(When more than one abbreviation appears with a cited work,
the additional abbreviations refer to commentaries on that work.)

Anonymous, *Agnipurāṇa*; Ānandāśrama Sanskrit Series 41
(1957)   AP

Appaya Dīkṣita, *Kuvalayānanda* (Bombay; Nirnaya Sagar
Press, 1955, tenth ed.); (with *Candrāloka*)

Arisiṃha, *Kāvyakalpalatā*; no edition available to annotator   AKK

Aśvaghoṣa, *Saundarananda*; ed. Johnston (London: Oxford
University Press, 1928)

Bāṇa, *Kādambarī*; ed. Kale (Bombay: Shāradākrīdan Press,
1896)

Bhāmaha, *Kāvyālaṃkāra*; appendix 8 to the *Pratāparudrayaśobhūṣaṇa* of Vidyānātha; Bombay Sanskrit Series 65   Bhām.

Bharata, *Nāṭyaśāstra*; Gaekwad Oriental Series; vol. 1 (36)
second ed., vol. 2 (68) first ed. (with a commentary of
Abhinavagupta)   Bhar. (NŚ), Abh. on NŚ (vol. 1 unless specified)

Bhartṛhari, *Vākyapadīya*; Benares Sanskrit Series 7 (1887)

Bhaṭṭa Lollata (commentator on Bharata, whose work is
now lost)

Bhaṭṭa Nāyaka, *Hṛdayadarpaṇa* (commentary or work based
on Bharata, now lost)

Bhavabhūti, *Mālatīmādhva* (Bombay: Nirnaya Sagar Press,
1936, sixth ed.)

Bhoja, *Sarasvatīkaṇṭhābharaṇa*; ed. Vidyāsāgara (Kalikāta:
Nārāyaṇayantre, 1894, second ed.)   BSKĀ

Bhoja, *Śṛṅgāraprakāśa*; unpublished   BŚP

Daṇḍin, *Kāvyādarśa*; ed. Bohtlingk (Leipzig: Haessel, 1890)   Dan.

De, S. K., *History of Sanskrit Literature* (University of
Calcutta, 1947)

De, S. K., *History of Sanskrit Poetics*, 2 vols. second ed. revised (Calcutta, 1960)   SKD HSP

Dhanañjaya, *Daśarūpaka* (Bombay: Nirnaya Sagar Press,
1941, fifth ed.)   DDR

Dhv., Ā on⎤ Dhavanikāra, *Dhvanyāloka* (with commentaries of Ānan-
Dhv., Abh.⎬ davardhana and Abhinavagupta); Kāvyamālā 25
on Dhv. ⎦

         Hemacandra, *Kāvyānuśāsana*; Kāvyamālā 71 (1934), second
HKA   ed.)
         Jagannātha, *Rasagaṅgādhāra*; Benares Sanskrit Series 8
JRGĀ   (1903)
         Jayadeva, *Candrāloka* (Bombay: Nirnaya Sagar Press,
         (1955); (with *Kuvalayānanda*)

         Kālidāsa, *Kumārasambhava* (Bombay: Nirnaya Sagar Press,
         1955, fourteenth ed.)
         Kālidāsa, *Raghuvaṃśa* (Bombay: Nirnaya Sagar Press, 1948,
         eleventh ed.)
         Kālidāsa, *Śakuntalā*, ed. Monier-Williams (Oxford: 1876)
         Kṣemendra, *Aucityavicāracarcā*, Kāvyamālā Gucchaka 1
AVC   (1886) 115–160
Kun   Kuntaka, *Kakroktijīvita* (Dillī: Ātmārām eṇḍ saṃs, 1955);
         pirated edition of Professor De's *Vakrotijīvita* (second
         ed.), which was not available to the annotator

         Māgha, *Śiśupālavadha* (Bombay: Nirnaya Sagar Press,
         1957, twelfth ed.)
         Mahimabhaṭṭa, *Vyaktiviveka*; Trivandrum Sanskrit Series
MVV   5 (1909)
         Mammaṭa, *Kāvyaprakāśa*; (with commentaries of Ṭhakkura
         and Vaidyanatha, called the "Prabhā"); *Kāvyamālā* 24
         (1891)
Mam. Abh.⎤ Mammaṭa, *Kāvyaprakāśa*; Ānandāśrama Sanskrit Series 66
[cited] ⎬ (1929); (with commentary of Govinda Ṭhakkura, called
by KPK   ⎦ the "Pradīpa"; Abhinavagupta quoted in extenso)

         Rāghavan V., *Some Concepts of Alankara Sastra* (Madras:
         Adyar, 1942)
         Rājaśekhara, *Kāvyamīmāṃsā*; Gaekwad Oriental Series 1
RKM   (1916)
         Renou, *L'Inde Classique* (Hanoi: 1953), vol. ii
         Rudrabhaṭṭa, *Śṛṅgāratilaka*; ed. Pischel (Kiel: Haeseler
RST   1886)
Rud.   Rudraṭa, *Kāvyālaṃkāra*; Kāvyamālā 2 (1928, third ed.)
UN   Rūpa Gosvāmin, *Ujjavalanīlamaṇi*; Kāvyamālā 95 (1913)
         Ruyyaka, *Alaṃkārasarvasva*; (with commentary of Samu-
         drabandha); Trivandrum Sanskrit Series 40 (1915)

Ruyyaka, *Alaṃkārasarvasva*; (with commentary of Jayaratha); Kāvyamālā 35 (1939, second ed.)   Ruy.

Śrīśaṅkuka (commentator on Bharata, whose work is now
lost)

Udbhaṭa, *Kāvyālaṃkārasārasaṃgraha;* Bombay Sanskrit
Series 79 (Poona: Aryabhushan Press, 1925)   Ud.

Vālmīki, *Rāmāyaṇa* (Gorakhpur: Gītā Press, n.d.)
Vāmana, *Kāvyālaṃkārasūtra(vṛtti)*; *Kāvyamālā* 15 (1953,
fourth ed.)   Vām.
Vidyādhāra, *Ekāvalī*; Bombay Sanskrit Series 63 (1903)   VEĀ
Vidyānātha, *Pratāparudrayaśobhūṣaṇa*; Bombay Sanskrit
Series 65 (1909)   VPR
Viśvanātha, *Sāhityadarpaṇa;* ed. Vidyāsāgara (Calcutta:
Mookerjee and Co., 1900)   VSD

TENTATIVE CHRONOLOGY

Pāṇini	fourth century B.C.?
Vālmīki	second century B.C.?
Aśvaghoṣa	first century A.D.
Kālidāsa	late fourth or early fifth century A.D.
Bāṇa	early seventh century
Bhartṛhari	first half of seventh century
Bharata	second to eighth centuries (text by the seventh)
Māgha	end of seventh
Bhāmaha	last quarter of seventh to middle of the eighth century
Bhavabhūti	first half of the eighth century
Daṇḍin	first half of the eighth century
Dhvanikāra	first half of the eighth century
Vāmana	middle of the eighth to middle of the ninth century (*ca.* 800)
Udbhaṭa	end of the eighth century into the ninth
Lollata	early ninth century?
Śrīśaṅkuka	first quarter of the ninth century
Rudraṭa	first quarter to the end of the ninth century
Ānandavardhana	middle of the ninth century
(*Agnipurāṇa*)	after the middle of the ninth century
Rājaśekhara	end of the ninth century through the early tenth
Nāyaka	last quarter of the ninth to last quarter of the tenth (earlier more likely)
Rudrabhaṭṭa	ninth through twelfth centuries, probably the tenth
Dhanañjaya	tenth century
Kuntaka	mid-tenth century to mid-eleventh century (earlier more likely)
Abhinavagupta	last quarter of the tenth to first quarter of the eleventh century

Bhoja	first half of the eleventh century
Kṣemendra	second and third quarters of the eleventh century
Mahimabhaṭṭa	last half or end of the eleventh century
Mammaṭa	mid-eleventh to first quarter of the twelfth century
Hemacandra	first three quarters of the twelfth century
Ruyyaka	second and third quarters of the twelfth century
Jayadeva	last quarter of the twelfth to first quarter of the fourteenth century
Arisiṃha	mid-thirteenth century
Vidyānātha	end of the thirteenth to early fourteenth century
Vidyādhāra	end of the thirteenth to early fourteenth century
Visvanātha	first half of the fourteenth century
Rupa Gosvāmin	second quarter of the sixteenth century
Appayya Dīkṣita	third and fourth quarters of the sixteenth century
Jagannātha	first half of the seventeenth century
V. Rāghavan	mid-twentieth century